Children of Earth
Part 3
Demon and the Saint

Henry Melton

Children of Earth
Part 3
Demon and the Saint

Henry Melton

Wire Rim Books
Hutto, Texas

WRB

Printing History
First Edition: November 2025
ISBN 978-1-935236-97-9

ePub ISBN 978-1-935236-99-3

Website of Henry Melton
www.HenryMelton.com

Printed in the United States of America

Wire Rim Books
www.wirerimbooks.com

Acknowledgements

As I bring the Project Saga to its conclusion with this Children of Earth trilogy, I'm grateful for the special early readers, some of which have been helping me from the beginning, decades ago. This time, it was a big ask, seeking help with three books at once.

Jim Dunn, Linda Elliott, Todd Hartman, Mike Lynch, Scott McNay, Tom Stock

Contents

Demon and the Saint

Injustice lasts a long time, even when people have a normal lifespan. When pain churns in an immortal heart, the results can be unthinkable. How long would it take to heal that pain? Is it even possible?

Beta in Ice

"I'm in the shadow." Jason Kidd muttered, flipping a manual switch just under the plain glass windshield. He squinted at the readouts on the panel. He shook his head at his foolishness. "I've got to stop talking to myself." It was a bad habit this personality had drifted into over the past year. Just another reason to retire this version of himself in a deadly accident and show up under another name in another place.

But he couldn't quit until he found her.

He peered intently out the window of the hopper as the small craft drifted slowly in the minuscule gravity across the Ceres landscape. Luckily the shadow he'd been thinking about was only the short range radio shadow that kept his activities pretty much hidden from the others in the expedition. The sun angle on the mostly black and white landscape gave him lots of contrast to look for any debris from the South Darnell impact hundreds of years ago. He wrinkled his nose. "Only three months in space and I'm already missing color."

It was the start of yet another space age. He'd missed the first one, back when there were rockets, but he'd been young enough to be excited about it when the Fleet went back into space. That was before he soured on the whole thing and tried to put a stop to humanity's expansion.

He'd never been comfortable about humans wielding enormous powers. He had stopped aging. He was immortal as long as no stupid ape dropped a rock on him.

There had been a close call when a beam accident sent tsunami across the Atlantic and nearly drowned him in the wash. He'd been perfectly justified in engineering a universal plague that shut it all down.

He'd hoped for more. He'd planned so put the human race back in the caves, with no more powerful weapons than stone axes, but that hadn't worked out. Civilization had collapsed. Space travel had ceased.

Maybe if he'd been in his right mind at the time he could have made it stick. But that didn't happen. Too many people survived, and some of them learned how to make those computers and spaceships live again.

The barricade had been lifted that had prevented any travel to and from Earth, and it wouldn't be long before every accessible planet, moon, or asteroid would be crawling with humans looking for a way to make some cash. Ceres, being one of the three big moons around Earth would be prime prospecting grounds, unless the revived Project put a stop to it. In the previous age, prior to the Plague, the Project had controlled all space travel. But now there was a lot of pushback from the new World Court, and they had substantial political say in the matter. This expedition to look for relics from the time of the Plague was a case in point.

In earlier ages, everything about it would be controlled by the Project.

This time, the collection of scholars from Bremerhaven University were doing it all, including piloting the hopper they were using to move around on the far side of Ceres.

Records from the Project said that Darnell Farms, an agricultural habitat, spinning in the Ceres Lagrangian cluster, was hit by a rogue beam and ruptured, causing it to split in two, tagged South Darnell and North Darnell. Jason was only interested in South Darnell, because of a brief message he'd received during the chaos. Beta, the female artificial human, his counterpart, had been on that doomed fragment. South Darnell had been steered into an impact on the uninhabited back side of Ceres. Computers left on automatic after the human controllers died had attempted to clean up any debris from the chaos that were a danger to Earth. Many of the destroyed space stations had been herded into safe collisions that way.

"What's that?" He tapped the controls on the hopper and eased closer to the mountains below. Ceres had no atmosphere to speak of, so impact features didn't weather. It was hard to know whether the scar was from part of the debris, or from a meteor a million years earlier. But there was something strange about it.

As he got closer, it was clear that it wasn't just one long scar, it was a string of them. Something relatively small had come in almost flat to the ground and clipped every rise and rock in its path. It didn't make any sense.

The Project data had given them the exact location where South Darnell had crashed. It looked like a hard impact, crushing and splintering everything as it came down. There was strong evidence of impact shock around the site. Still, it wasn't all vaporized. The expedition was crawling all over the rubble, looking for anything recognizable. Nobody had seen a corpse. The consensus was that Darnell had been evacuated before it split. Of the twenty people in the search crew, a vocal minority were ready to move on to the next crash site. They'd only come to South Darnell first because Jason had put himself in place to modify the agenda. Other crash sites were more likely to have been populated to the last.

The computer lit up. "Message for Jason Kidd."

He sighed. It was the expedition coordinator, a thorn in his side. "I'm here."

There was a noticeable delay. The message was probably relayed from Luna, just barely visible on the horizon.

"Did you steal the hopper again?"

"Just following up on a lead. I'm looking for splash debris."

"Well, get back here! August discovered an apple tree! A real vacuum-frozen apple tree, complete with baby apples. He wants to use the hopper to haul it back to base camp."

"As soon as I can. I'm following up on a discovery myself. At least, I hope it's one. I'll get back to you."

There was another reply, but Jason let it blink. An apple tree was hardly surprising, at least to him. He had a centuries-old memory of eating a Darnell apple, back when he visited space a few times. It was a little surprising which memories could be triggered when he had so many of them. Being a genetically constructed immortal had its uncharted territory. He was the only one of his kind—at least the only one now. Beta had been on the fractured station and there was no way she had survived.

He brought the hopper down to nearly ground level and lined up along the scars. Off in the distance, there was another blemish. He followed.

Irrational hope nagged at him. Could she have escaped the crash of South Darnell? He knew that if he were in that situation he'd have made every effort to dodge death. Just being in a body that didn't age didn't protect you from injuries.

The next scar looked like a track, rather than an impact. He slowed the hopper to walking pace and followed the wide depression until it vanished into a crevice. Due to the sun angle, it was pitch black down in the crack. He settled the hopper down on the edge and aimed a light, sweeping the depths. There was something down there.

The crevice was too tight quarters for the hopper. He'd have to climb down for a closer look. His spacesuit was rugged, designed for exploring on asteroids. With the weak gravity, he had no worry about getting trapped down there.

He lit up the head-mounted lights and eased down into the depths. *Could she have ...?*

But it wasn't any kind of craft. Just a heavily dented water tank with a cable tangled around it. *Is that ice?*

It was clear that water had sprayed out of the tank even after it had crashed on the surface. Protected from sunlight, the ice had survived in the darkness. He eased closer, careful to avoid any sharp rocks or metal shards.

The light caught her profile, just visible under the ice.

"Beta!" He gasped. Had she cobbled together an escape pod out of a water tank and managed a soft landing on Ceres? It had to be her. Normal humans weren't that smart.

His hand shook as he reached out to touch the ice. Just the light pressure of his glove shook the ice and a piece separated from the rest. He winced as he realized the whole mass was riddled with cracks. Her frozen body had likely shattered as well.

Beta had struggled to escape an impossible situation, making her own escape craft when there was nothing for her. But even if she had managed to survive the landing riding a water-venting tank, she'd never have been able to survive on the barren surface of Ceres.

"But so close! So close! You did good, girl!"

The Jason Kidd persona had never been emotional, so the tears felt strange. He blinked them away.

It was clear there'd be no chance of thawing her out and reviving her. Still, his mind raced. He'd need to confirm this was Beta through genetic analysis, but there was plenty of well-preserved tissue. Could he grow a clone of her?

The Old Man persona, normally quiet in the back recesses of his mind, said, "Of course I can do it."

Jason's mind raced. There was so much to do. He had to free her from the ice, pack her body in the hopper and make sure nobody else on the expedition discovered her.

"It's definitely time Jason Kidd had his accident."

. . .

Sir Ohen Barclay glanced at his passengers and then guided his landing craft, the B3, through the narrow canyon that made up Stampz Gate. The gasps at the view on the screen were all that he'd hoped for as they raced between the rock walls. He had taken the gap at higher speeds in the past, but the shock wave of his passage had caused complaints from the travelers on the road below and he had to stop doing that.

Still, the passengers had seen amazing sights in space and he needed something to impress them as they visited Luna. The drop down from space had been nothing more than endless clouds whipping by.

As the canyon opened up and they saw their destination in the distance, Kerry, the white-haired healer chuckled. She smiled. "I take it that your princess lives in that fairytale castle up ahead?"

"Yes, our place is on the fifth floor, but most of the time she's down in the library. That's in an underground floor that's been carved out to hold all the books. They like to keep the air at a constant temperature and humidity to protect the pages." Ohen liked to remind them that his wife was more than just her royal title.

The short-range radio spoke. "B-three landing approved on the south field. Happy to see you back Sir Ohen."

"They're having you do landing control today, Abraham?"

"Well, yes. I had a day off from my classes so I got assigned to this once your call came in."

"Sorry about that. I'm not going anywhere soon, so this should be the last of it."

The chief pilot and instructor for the World Court Pilot Training Academy sighed. "You never can tell. There's just too many ships in the sky these days."

Ohen chuckled. "It'll only get worse."

"I know. I just miss the days when I was the only space ship pilot in the whole Solar system. And then you came along."

"Sorry. Making my turn. I hope the field is clear."

"Should be, but watch for stray livestock."

They both laughed at the memory of trying to land on top of a stampeding herd of cattle a couple of years earlier. Grassy meadows made great landing fields, but also good grazing land.

Kerry and Gabriel were watching the screen, and likely scanning the field with their own clairvoyant senses. The third passenger, John, seemed relaxed and disinterested in the landing details. Ohen had his suspicions about the man, but there'd never been time alone with him to ask the right questions.

The U'tanse; Kerry bar Trask, Gabriel bar Rush, and of course, Ohen bar Clay himself were all telepaths. The other passenger was John Lupin, a paying passenger from the Americas on Earth.

The reason Ohen had his doubts was that John appeared to be one of those rare natural humans who could keep his thoughts concealed under an untrained ineda. Ohen had told the U'tanse that he had met several people who to some extent could block their thoughts. Since telepathy among normal humans was extremely rare, no Earth humans had ever formalized telepathy-blocking ineda training—he had been surprised that it existed at all.

The only other walking talking person Ohen had ever met who didn't radiate any of their thoughts wasn't really human at all. Could Lupin be one of those?

But once they settled onto the grass, there was no time for idle speculation. Ohen said, "Give me a moment to match the atmosphere. I've been gradually adjusting the pressure since I picked up John at Ceres, but let me even out the last percent before I open the doors."

Lupin immediately began collecting his bags and making sure everything was sealed up. Kerry and Gabriel followed his example, although they only had a single bag apiece.

The airlocks opened and Kerry took a deep breath. "What is that smell?" She hurried out, eager to see the new world. Gabriel was right behind her.

Ohen said, "Mr. Lupin, there will be people to help with your sample cases."

The merchant nodded. "That would be helpful."

Outside, Kerry was down on her knees in the grass. Gabriel was jumping around in the low gravity.

"You've got to try this," Gabriel yelled. Ohen just waved his hand.

Lupin shook his head, trying to keep from bouncing as he walked. "I've had low-gravity training, but I'm not going to make the best impression on potential trading partners with a broken leg."

Kerry asked, "Ohen, how did they manage to plant all these?"

"Nobody planted the grass. The wind and the animals disperse the seeds. And believe me, Lunar winds are quite capable of carrying seeds across the globe." He pointed, "But avoid those."

She froze and pulled her hand back from the flat item near her. "Why?"

"Animal excrement. Cattle graze in the grass and litter the place with them."

She sighed. "There's so much I don't know about planetary ecologies. It's not at all like living in space."

"You'll be living here for a couple of months at least, and there's a lot you can learn." He didn't mention her real reason for being here—monitoring Ohen and Alice's sex life and coaching Ohen on how to cull any semen that would give them a telepathic child. It wasn't something he wanted to be overheard.

Gabriel shouted, "A vehicle is approaching!" He landed with a double bounce, breathing hard.

Ohen nodded. "Previously, ships landed very close to the castle, but with land prices so high, they made us use this field. Part of the deal was transportation for luggage and cargo." He grinned. "Plus, the guards like to get a good look at all the strangers who come to visit."

Kerry grinned. "They don't trust us?"

Ohen shook his head. "They don't trust anyone. Too many spies over the years. The guards don't even trust the locals half the time."

Gabriel lifted his ineda for just an instant to let a telepathic thought through. **I have my questions about Lupin.**

Ohen frowned. Gabriel tightened up his telepathic block and looked away. They shouldn't even discuss certain things via thought. Just because Ohen had never met a telepath among the natural humans didn't mean they didn't exist. A secret should remain a secret.

A wagon pulled by an ox approached with three men jogging along ahead of it. Ohen smiled when he saw his wife riding with the driver.

When she got closer, she smiled at him, then called out to the white-haired healer playing in the grass.

"Kerry bar Trask! The grass will stain your clothes if you aren't careful!"

The woman hurriedly looked at her leggings and brushed at her knees, then sighed. "I hope it washes out."

Ohen stepped up to the wagon and held out his hand to Alice. "I probably should have warned them, but they were having so much fun."

He whispered in her ear, "And if we finally get children out of this, then we'll have much more fun than we know how to handle."

The Perfect Boyfriend

Jason Kidd frowned, seeing a small fishing boat off in the waters of Canal Chiriaco just off the cliffs of Isla Teresa.

There shouldn't be any humans in the Archipiélago de los Chronos, although from what he could see through his small viewport carved into the stone wall they just appeared to be fishing.

Were the merpeople losing their reputation for sinking ships so quickly? Maybe the local Chileans had made a deal with them that he didn't know about.

I've got to stop being Jason Kidd!

He closed his eyes and reverted to the Paul Santos persona. He shuttered the opening facing the Pacific to prevent any light leaks and went back to the lab. Moving like a man in his mid-forties, he scratched at his right temple and peered at the computer display.

From the body of Beta, he had retrieved a hundred cell samples. Comparing full genetic profiles, sixty-three had shown to have un-degraded DNA from the original. He froze half of those and the remaining were undergoing the revitalization process that were turning them into progenitor cells that could develop into embryos. He would be checking the DNA each step of the process to weed out any latent problems. He wanted an identical copy of Beta, not a mutation.

The process was spelled out in the genetic textbooks archived at this secret military base. The Chileans had plans to secretly use the technology that had been banned after King Thomas's War. Agents had scoured the

Australian continent after the war ended and only abandoned their plans when the anti-genetic fervor proved deep and long-lasting.

He had discovered records that hinted at the existence of this abandoned facility back when he was formulating his plan to knock humanity back to the stone age and take all their dangerous toys away from them. Back then, he had access to airships and the resources to reactivate the hidden base and use it for his own projects.

It had been more difficult to get here this time. While he remembered at least two TP powered airships hidden in secret locations, the whole world was alert to the possibility of ships coming from the other planets now. Before the Plague, he could blend in with all the other air traffic, but during the long centuries when Earth couldn't get any more charged power cells from space, air travel dwindled to nothing. From time to time people would dig out the plans for the petroleum-powered craft of ancient times, but since the petrochemical energy was long gone, only the alcohol-powered aircraft were ever built. At least for now, any kind of aircraft would be too noticeable.

Shipping the pieces of Beta's frozen body to Puerto Montt in three sealed containers via separate routes had been difficult, but it was a task he'd perfected over the ages. Jason Kidd then had his "accident" in a small boat lost in the South Pacific, supposedly a few hundred miles from Concepción and the body was never recovered.

Paul Santos, who had been nothing more than a few database entries for decades, then arrived to receive the containers.

The smuggling industry had found ways around the merpeople's shipping restrictions and Paul purchased a small hydrofoil craft to make the last run to the secret base in the hidden islands. Jason Kidd, the merpeople's advocate for so many years, knew where the merfolk patrolled and where they didn't. Clear passages could be found. He arrived at the hidden dock on Isla Teresa with no issues and the rest was just hard work getting the base reactivated and Beta's body safely protected in the freezers.

It was a lot of work, single-handedly doing the job of a whole crew of scientists and technicians. There were dozens of machines running, analyzing and processing the samples. What he was trying to do wasn't something the Chileans had anticipated, but it wasn't too different. The machines could handle it, but he needed to control every step of the process himself.

As the number of viable samples dwindled, he started to worry that he might have to go back to Beta's frozen body parts and harvest even more.

Inserting the cell nuclei into body cells he had taken from himself was the most difficult step. When the final results showed seven completed embryonic cells beginning to divide into multi-cell embryos, he finally breathed a sigh of relief. Carefully, he froze them for storage.

For the next stage he needed a host, a mother.

· · ·

Paul Santos used winches to hoist his hydrofoil into the protective shed on the coast, the same one where he'd had Beta's remains shipped originally, just a few hours down the road from Concepción. In the doorway, he paused and stared at the water.

His face changed. Just a few muscles relaxed and he looked like a man in his twenties again. His Paul Santos identification went into a hidden pouch in his backpack and he made sure his wallet proclaimed him to be Juan Ramos.

Juan smiled and stepped out onto the road. It would be a little hike before he reached his new residence, an apartment near the Bio Bio River in the heart of the city. He needed the exercise. Tending the machines as Paul had stiffened him up.

Concepción was hardly a major city, but it was large enough that he could be lost in the crowds and besides, he loved the wordplay of having his new daughter born in this place. If he needed to make another trip back to the hidden base, it was close enough to make the trip with only a single tank of alcohol. There were hardly any refueling places on this sparsely populated stretch of the Pacific coast. Most of alcohol production went to electric generation and rail lines, and only cities like Concepción were in the loop.

Juan had seen technology shifts before. Opening up spaceflight would quickly bring cheaper energy than the alcohol plants could produce. It might be worthwhile to make a few timely investments. He could always use more money.

As he walked, he noticed a bus and numerous individuals on noisy scooters. The alcohol economy wouldn't collapse suddenly, not as long as there was infrastructure that had that need built in. But maybe he should be alert for someone to buy his hydrofoil while he could get a good price.

Still, that was a job for another day.

He quickly found his apartment building and received his access code from the manager. The room was bare. The bed had nothing covering the mattress. The bathroom had no towels. It was at least clean, but it had been stripped of everything portable.

Taking a few minutes to shower and air-dry himself, he headed out to do some shopping.

. . .

Her name tag proclaimed her Viviana. Juan smiled and she smiled back. The shop had a few items he needed, and more importantly, the freshly baked pastries called to him.

"If you eat any more of those, you'll get fat."

He shook his head. "I never get fat."

She patted her stomach. "Well, I'm jealous."

Juan shook his head. "A few more pounds wouldn't hurt you in the least."

And he meant it. He was on the lookout for young females that were potential mothers for the new Beta, both in personality and body. Since he would have to seduce the girl, he had chosen the Juan persona, who over the centuries had charmed a number of fair maidens. Viviana would do nicely.

One row over, in the dry goods, a surly teen griped, "Quit flirting with the customers!"

Juan whispered, "Your brother?"

She shook her head. "Son of the owner. Sometimes he thinks he's in charge."

Juan changed the topic to his bare apartment and asked for help locating some place to buy towels and bedding. She offered to help, once she got off of her shift.

. . .

He picked her up in his rental cargo trike and they visited a few stores together before returning to his apartment. She was shocked that it was just as bare as he had said and had many suggestions on how to make the place more livable.

Juan was quick to compliment her on her ideas and had her delivered safe and sound to her boarding house before her curfew.

She sighed, easing out of the seat. They had been very close together on the ride. "It would be nice to live in an apartment on my own, but my folks wouldn't even let me move to the city without making their own arrangements."

They made plans to meet up again the next day. Juan was satisfied at his progress. When she moved in with him, she'd be positive that it was all her idea.

. . .

It took a week, but she spent the night at his apartment and he took the opportunity to lightly drug her and perform a detailed physical exam. She woke in the morning with no hint of what had happened to her. She was more concerned with getting to her job on time and how she would make her excuses at the boarding house.

Juan began the process of preparing the embryo for implantation.

He began telling Viviana about the job he had, expanding the rail transport system along the Pacific coast, preparing her for his occasional travel days. She was in the early stages of infatuation and fretted over being apart from him.

By the second week of their affair, he was focused on supporting her as she contacted her parents to explain the notice the boarding house had sent them. Her parents were angry and he was her refuge.

If there was one thing he had learned over his lifespan, it was patience. It nagged at him, day by day, as he hoped for some sign that she was pregnant.

But the day came and she had her regular period. He hid his disappointment. She had no idea what was going on and wouldn't understand.

. . .

On his next "work trip", he made a race back to the hidden base to pull another embryo out of cold storage. He hoped that with his better knowledge of her ovarian cycle that the second attempt would be successful. Engineering a break up and finding another host mother would be difficult, and probably impossible in Concepción. Relocating would be a drain on his resources, but trying to get Viviana pregnant if she wasn't for some reason compatible with Beta's embryos was a bad idea as well.

Still Juan was a good actor and a cheerful and supportive friend to the girl. She was out of her depth, risking it all for a man who seemed so perfect. He knew how to play that role and he intended to make no mistakes for the next couple of years.

A few weeks later, Juan knew the signs before Viviana did. When she started looking pensive, and then forced herself to be bright and cheerful, he knew she was getting her body's signals.

Three days later, Viviana fixed a wonderful fish dinner, officially for their three-month anniversary. When he complimented her, raving about how great a cook she was, she blushed and hesitantly mentioned that she wondered if there was a reason she had been having indigestion recently.

"I might even be pregnant."

Juan took her hand. "Really. We can test for that, you know. I'd love to have a little one."

She sighed, letting out the tension. "I already checked. I am pregnant."

He swept her up in a hug. "That's wonderful. I'm so glad."

He met her eyes. "I've been thinking about it, but I haven't gotten the nerve to bring it up—but we should be married! Would you do me the honor of becoming my wife?"

. . .

They made a trip to Curacautin in the mountains to meet Viviana's parents, William and Estelle Garza, and gave them the good news. The marriage was only two weeks later, and her father gave his grudging approval.

Juan was deeply involved in the pre-natal care and changed his job, ostensibly so that he wouldn't have to travel and be away from her when she needed help.

Things went smoothly until it was clear that nine months had come and gone. The doctor shrugged and said that sometimes it just took longer for some babies. Juan made up a story that he had been a late baby himself, although he really had no records of that. Any documentation about the Alpha and Beta children were totally scrubbed when the original researchers tried to escape the anti-genetic purge after King Thomas's war.

Still, considering how slowly he matured, it wasn't too surprising that gestation took longer as well. He tried to comfort Viviana when she worried that something was wrong with her daughter.

But at about ten months, perfect little Billie was born. Juan was happy to name her a "B" name but said it was to make grandpa William happy.

In all the relationships Alpha had over the centuries, very few of them were with women who had children and only a couple had infants. Juan fumbled through diaper changes and grumbled when Billie cried. Viviana took to motherhood naturally and for several months, they had a happy little home—unless Billie was acting up.

But her slow growth was worrisome. It was reaching the point where the little baby girl was still physically an infant, but she was starting to say "Mamma".

Viviana whispered to Juan in the bed. "I'm worried. I think maybe we should find a doctor who can check to see if she has any hormone problems or things like that."

Juan gave her a hug. "Oh, I don't think there's anything wrong. I know I heard tales that I developed slowly myself. Billie just probably inherited that from me."

"I'm really worried. I'd feel a lot better if a doctor did some tests."

Juan sighed. "Okay, I'll ask around. I want one good doctor rather than a dozen local guys who don't really specialize in child development. Give me some time to plan it out."

"Okay."

. . .

From Bahía de San Vicente around the rocky Punta Ballenera and up the river to downtown Concepción was a fun excursion that Juan talked up for a week before Viviana gave in. They boarded the boat with over sixty passengers and started up. Juan had a new carrying bag for little Billie and he tucked her in carefully. Mom was grateful she wasn't on carry duty for the day, that is until she got a little seasick in the rough waves.

"You just stay put here on the bench until you feel better. I've got some bread to let Billie feed the seagulls. Just rest."

Viviana smiled through her discomfort. Juan turned his back on her and walked out on the deck. He had to be in just the right position.

He rested against the railing and fed Billie a special candy. Her eyes closed in a few seconds and he tucked her into her carrying bag, opened the valve on the concealed air bottle and sealed the waterproof opening.

One minute later, there was the sharp groan of abused metal and the excursion boat shifted hard over to starboard. There were screams as a dozen people fell overboard. Juan and Billie were right in the water with them. Juan slipped a swim mask over his eyes and carried the both of them deeper and away from the boat.

There was a high-pitched noise that Juan could barely hear, but he was expecting it. The tour boat company had advertised that their vessels were equipped with emergency alarms. The merfolk made extra money from time to time rescuing people lost at sea. Juan was grateful. If the ship alarm hadn't sounded, he'd have had to call them himself.

Juan spent the next few minutes keeping their distance from the other flailing passengers. And then, a sturdy young merman showed up. Juan triggered a pre-recorded message in the merfolk language, "These are the words of WhaleRider, leader of the Volcano Nation. Take this human where he wants to go and claim a boon from the Council."

Hardly any human could read the expression on the face of a merman, but Juan could. The young warrior looked shocked at the words and then overjoyed. A boon from the Council wasn't anything that could be ignored.

Juan made a hand gesture and they linked arms. Powerful swimming muscles pulled the land dweller and his precious bundle rapidly through the water. Only a dozen stops for air and gestured directions and then Juan was safely out of sight at his dock. Billie in her bag was still asleep and breathing calmly. He'd be heading north on his hydrofoil as soon as it was dark. Viviana, if she was unharmed, would make plenty of noise to look for her family, but the mermen would only be interested in the money for the tourists they had rescued. In the whole world, there were only four translators for the merpeople, none in South America. There had been five before Jason Kidd had "died". No one would be able to question them about Juan.

He already had documents for his new identity and a fresh birth certificate for Billie with her original birth date suitably adjusted. Far to the north, he'd surely be able to charm another mother to take the poor motherless infant under her wing.

Who knew how many families he'd have to make and break until Billie was capable of living without a mother, but he'd lived that way centuries ago, as had the original Beta. He was sure she could handle it.

The Galactics Arrive

Sammy Barclay yelled down at his daddy, "The wagon's coming!"

Sir Ohen waved back at his four-year-old. Just a year ago, little Sammy had stopped complaining about the high gravity workouts when he realized he could jump higher than any of his friends. Since then he was always climbing up on the roofs of buildings and exploring his limits.

Bringing his infant son along for the full-gravity family workouts on his boat had just been a whim. His son would never be a telepath like he was, but other than that, he didn't want him to suffer any disadvantage in his adult life. He'd thought that someday his son might want to travel to the other planets and people who grew up in lunar gravity were always at a disadvantage. The high gravity never hurt—humans were genetically designed for a full gravity after all.

Ohen hadn't realized that the day was coming sooner than he had imagined.

Alice came out the door from their five-story house, the baby bump just barely visible in her library robes. "Is Sammy up on the roof again?"

"He's playing lookout. The wagon is coming. He's all excited at getting to come along on the trip."

Alice put her palm on her belly. "I hope we're not making a mistake."

"We really don't know how long this will take. Better to bring the whole family along. I'd hate to be separated for a couple of years."

"I hope it's not that long. I'd rather Helen be born on Luna."

Ohen smiled. "I still prefer Clarissa over Helen."

Alice shrugged. "We still have a few months to make the final decision."

Everything they'd planned now had to be rescheduled. The Galactics had arrived and representatives from Luna and the U'tanse had to drop everything to make their presentations. Little things like raising a family were forced down on the priority list.

She waited with clenched teeth as Sammy climbed down the outside of the building, making an easy drop from windowsill to windowsill. She hoped the Galactics were ready for Sammy.

"The wagon is just over the hill."

Alice said, "Okay, run in and tell Maggie to bring out the luggage."

Sammy grinned, happy that he got away with his climb without being scolded.

Ohen checked again, as he always did, making sure that there was no hint that Sammy had any telepathic sense. The boy didn't have a hint that such a thing was even possible. Ohen was grateful and sad at the same time. The only place telepathic children could grow up sane was in the carefully controlled U'tanse culture, and his son was a native of Luna, in mainstream humanity.

. . .

"What's that?" Sammy was pointing at the boat's display as they approached their destination.

Ohen asked, "Which one? The big one, or the one with a hole in it?"

The boy shook his head. "All of them!"

Ohen smiled. "The one that looks like a donut is a place where people stay. It spins and makes gravity for everyone. The big one next to it is the Galactic starship."

"Where all the monsters live?"

"They're not monsters—just people that look different."

Sammy put out his lower lip. "No monsters? Maggie said that there would be monsters."

Ohen frowned. He'd need to have a word with the servants when they returned home.

"No, the real monsters are like the bears that live outside of Stampz crater."

Sammy was disappointed because he'd told his best friend Jerry that he was going to go visit monsters. Hopefully he'd see something to suitably impress his friends.

"The smaller dots are boats like ours that are bringing people from all the different worlds. We'll be staying on the donut with the others. There are a lot of people that have to meet with the Galactics."

"Where is home?" He sounded a little uncertain.

"Come here to the controls." He coached Sammy's little fingers over the buttons and the image scanned to the side where Earth and Luna were visible.

"It looks smaller now."

"We're farther away. We've traveled a long distance."

They'd been watching Luna shrink in size on the trip and Sammy was getting use to the idea that his whole world could be just a small circle of light in the distance. He'd been disappointed when he couldn't even see his home crater once they took off from Stampz and entered the first cloud layer.

But once they docked and carried their bags on board the Grand Mariana Hotel and registered for rooms on the inner ring with the lowest gravity, Sammy was overjoyed to discover the holographic images in the main lobby.

Someone had made full sized images of the main races aboard the Galactic starship.

"That's a big bug."

Ohen said, "That's what we call a Click. They made the starships. They are people."

Sammy nodded slowly, a little reluctant to get close to the iridescent blue, beetle-like body with four arms. It was about the size of a pony and looked like it could run fast.

"Can you read the sign?"

Sammy struggled. Alice had been teaching him to read since he was three, but he struggled to get through the words. Ohen helped him when the description got technical.

They walked through the displays. The Kwish looked like three-meter-long dolphins with arms and hands that recessed into long body cavities.

The Nuren were humanoid with large eyes, not too much taller than Sammy. The description said that they were often the prime investigator for physics-based inventions. They wore clothes and their skin appeared to be a pale green.

Sammy said, "I want a hat like that."

Alice said, "Draw a picture and probably John can make you one when we get home." Luna was nearly always cloudy, with a thick atmosphere and hats were only used for wind and rain protection. The Nuren seemed to have one that shielded its eyes from the bright light of alien suns.

"They're fuzzy!" Sammy frowned at the pair of Hurf in the next exhibit.

Alice asked, "What's wrong?"

Sammy asked, "Which way are they facing?"

"Well, let's read about them."

The Hurf were an extremely social race that were often the primary contact for new alien races. They were radially symmetrical, four-footed beings about as tall as they were wide, covered in hair that not only changed color at will, but also could be waved rapidly enough to make a humming noise. They always moved in groups and were never found alone.

Sammy struggled with the symmetry issue, but was looking forward to meeting the Hurf in real life.

"Sammy, just because they look fluffy, doesn't mean you can pet them. You wouldn't want one of the Click to come up and pet you without warning, do you?"

Supposedly, there were other species aboard the starship, but the first contact team hadn't been able to see them and the Galactics weren't really forthcoming with information that didn't interest them.

Eventually, they made their way up to their room. Sammy had to be stopped from jumping on the bed.

Alice stretched out. "This is Mars gravity?"

Ohen nodded. "It's the best they could do. Just be glad we've been doing our workouts."

"What's it going to be like on the Galactic's starship?"

"Supposedly, they have customized floor gravity, too. We can always ask."

. . .

Their apartment in Cartagena was comfortable, but not luxurious. Every time Alpha and Billie had to die and move on, he was always leaving money behind.

There was a light tap on the door.

"Come in."

Billie pushed the heavy door to his study open and put all her weight behind her to close it with a click. She straightened up, walking more confidently when alone with her father than she ever did with other people. She had internalized the role she was playing, pretending to be much younger than her real age.

"Daddy, what do you know about these Galactics everyone is talking about?"

He leaned back in his chair. "It's certainly nothing a two-year-old should be talking about."

She sniffed. "I know that! But just how serious is it?"

He shook his head. "It's no problem on the short term. They aren't bringing armies to conquer the Earth. All they want to do is trade. If it works out, then maybe we'll get something new, like starships. If it all falls apart, then the Galactics will go away and leave us alone."

Billie frowned, trying to make sense of it. She was much more intelligent than her actual age. The both of them had been engineered to be smarter than any human on the planet. She loved the times she could sneak into Daddy's office and talk with him alone. Everyone else, even the adults, seemed slow to her. It was obvious that what he'd told her—that they were different from regular people—was true.

It also made perfect sense that she should pretend to be a two-year-old for while longer.

"Daddy, Susan is looking at me funny."

He nodded. "Has she said anything?"

"She's stopped using baby talk. I think she knows I understand everything."

"Hmm. Have you tried calling her Momma? You know she wants that."

Billie looked stubborn. "It's not worth it. How many Momma's have I had? It's hard on me when I get too close and then it's time to leave."

"I'm sorry about that. Maybe next time you can dress older and we can go with the story that you're a midget with some genetic difference that makes you smaller."

She wrinkled her nose. "Maybe. Isn't it the point to pretend to be normal?"

He shrugged. "I tried the small-person story a couple of times when I was young. The real issue is staying healthy and never having a reason to get a medical checkup. People can accept genius kids more easily than they can get along with genius adults. The danger is when there's a big disconnect between the mental age you show and the physical age you appear.

"It will be easier when you appear older and act a little younger so you can approach normal."

She pouted. "When will I ever get to the point where I can just be myself and nobody cares?"

He just shook his head. "Humans will always attack the strange ones. That's why I'm just watching this Galactics business from a distance. It would be idiotic for humans to offend a collection of races much more powerful than they are, but I don't have any faith that humans won't still be idiots."

"I hope they don't attack me."

He waved at the shelves in his office. "That's why we should never talk about our differences in any other place. Nobody can hear what we say in here. There's hardly anyone in the world that can even imagine a person with different genetics. They can't imagine our real differences, so they always make their own excuses when we do something they don't expect. I've done so many dangerous things in my life and gotten away with it because nobody believes what they see."

He frowned as he watched little Billie thinking about what he'd said. He pointed at her. "But don't you think you can start being dangerous. Not yet. People will instinctively try to stop small children from hurting themselves. Nobody will have any confidence in your abilities."

Frustration and Boredom

Sammy put his hand to his mouth. Diplomats, not even children of diplomats, were not suppose to laugh at other people. Momma had been very clear about that and he'd be in big trouble if he let it out.

But when the small furry Hurfs, all five of them, addressed the visitors at the diplomatic party, sounding like a big male human, with a strong, deep, resonant voice, it really looked and sounded funny. Sammy caught part of the message. The Galactics had excellent speech translation software and they were already familiar with English from talking with the U'tanse.

The rest of the message was boring, so Sammy started looking at the other humans. People dressed funny on other worlds. While almost all of them were diplomats or scientists, there were a couple of children there as well. He caught the eye of an older girl, obviously the daughter of that couple with her. She looked back and waved a few fingers his way, trying not to look too bored by the long speech. Sammy liked the way her hair was tied up in braids. Braids were popular on Luna. He wondered if she lived in a place that had strong winds, too.

After the speech, there was yet another part of the party where people wandered around and talked. Only this one had Hurf and Nuren in the mix.

"No Clicks?" Sammy asked.

His mother heard him, but waved her hand sideways. She was busy talking to some diplomat from some place on Earth called Africa. He took that as permission to wander around. A few cautious steps later without being called back, he grew more confident.

The girl with the braids was in a group close to the Hurf. He moved up close to them.

One of the Hurf was the spokesperson, answering some question about how the Hurf lived on their planet.

The girl leaned close to Sammy and whispered, "Are you a tag-along, too?"

He nodded. "Sammy, from Luna."

"Lexi. My parents are in the North American delegation."

Sammy whispered, "I saw a Nuren, too. Have you seen a Click?"

She shook her head.

But the Hurf must have heard their whispers. "There are only Hurf and Nuren in this meeting. The Click are not social, although they will be participants in some of the technical evaluations. The Kwish are, of course, limited to their water environments."

Lexi blushed at having been overheard. Sammy tried to keep from giggling. She took his hand and led them out of the group so they wouldn't interrupt the adults.

"How old are you?" she asked.

"I'll be five in Jule."

"July?"

"Jule, the month. Oh! Lunar days are 48 hours long. We have a different calendar."

"Well, anyway, you're large for your age."

Sammy smiled. "My family. You can always spot my Daddy in a crowd. He's tall."

Lexi nodded, not really interested. "Have you seen the observation lounge?"

"No."

"Want to? They'll be talking for hours."

Sammy looked back at the crowd. Daddy was with some scientists. Mommy was talking with a different group. He could sneak out for a while.

Lexi led the way to the elevators. The observation lounge was near the hub. There was a small area with a big screen focused on Earth. Lexi hurried up close to the screen and peered closely. "It looks clear over Chicago."

"Is that your country?"

She smiled back at Sammy. "No, silly. Chicago is the capital of the Great Lakes Economic Zone. That's where I'm from."

Sammy came closer and saw that it wasn't really a window, just a larger version of the display like on his Daddy's boat. "Is that good?"

Lexi smiled. "Oh, yes. Since the merpeople never moved into the Great Lakes, we could still have shipping and such and a lot of the continent's industry is centered around there."

Sammy looked and found the buttons like the ones Daddy had taught him to use on the boat. He pressed one and the image shifted.

"What did you do?" Lexi asked.

"Moved the image." He tapped a button and the image of Earth jumped away, looking like a tiny distant station.

"Bring it back!" Lexi looked around, afraid someone would appear and send them away.

"Okay. What do you want to look at?"

"Chicago. Can you do that?"

He brought the image closer. "Show me where." She pointed and he steered the controls until they brought the city so close it shifted and blurred because of the atmosphere.

"I can't get it any better."

Lexi stared longingly at her home town. "You're a smart kid, Sammy."

"Daddy lets me use the computer."

"That's lucky. We don't have one yet."

She kept staring at the far-away image. "How long do you think we'll have to stay here? I miss my friends."

Sammy shrugged. "I overheard my parents talking. I'm only here because they didn't want me to be alone for years."

"Surely not years!"

"They gotta sell the Galactics some kind of technology and it might take a long time. Momma was worried my baby sister will be born here."

Lexi frowned. "I can't stay here that long."

. . .

It was a long time.

Sammy's chores increased once baby Helen was born. He even got to sit in the back of the council meetings, since somebody had to rock the baby and both of his parents had important things to say at those meetings.

The hunt for some human invention to sell to the Galactics was not going well. He could see that in the conversations. The adults were frustrated, and it showed in these human-only meetings.

Momma explained it. Bad aliens, not the Galactics, had tried to attack Earth and crashed. People found the engines and humans just thought they had invented the engines themselves, but it really belonged to the Galactics all along. Now they wanted the humans to either stop using the engines that powered everything or come up with some invention that the other aliens hadn't already invented for themselves.

It was impossible to stop using the engines. For one thing Daddy's boat used them and they'd never get home to grandfather's castle. This big spinning wheel was a fun place to explore, but home was better.

Daddy was talking. "We've gotten permission from Project Command. They'll be moving one of the big projectors here for the Nuren to crawl through and examine. It's still based on the TP license, but it sounds like none of the other races has scaled it up where we were, moving moons around and terraforming planets. Maybe we can convince the Galactics that we've invented something new here."

Sammy knew what he'd be doing when that happened. He was an expert at using the observation lounge display. He'd helped adults find their home, both on Earth and Mars. He wanted to see the big TP projector Daddy was talking about.

After the meeting his parents were discussing the meeting.

Momma was cradling baby Helen and sighed. "It's getting pretty desperate. I've heard that some of the other delegations are giving up."

Sammy popped up. "It's true. Lexi said her parents were going back to Chicago in another few days. She go excited to go back to her friends. She just doesn't think it's that important to make the Galactics happy."

She shifted Helen to the other side and asked, "Sammy, what do you think? Are you sorry your friend is leaving?"

"Lexi is happy. There's a guy back in Chicago she's always talking about. Her father gets mad when she's too friendly with the workers here on the station."

"And you? Are you lonely without your friends?"

Sammy shrugged. He wasn't going to admit that, nor reveal that Luke in grandfather's castle and he had been secretly exchanging messages over the computer for a couple of months.

He changed the subject. "Daddy's U'tanse people are always wanting to talk to me. Did you know my U'tanse name isn't Sammy Barclay, it's Samuel bar Ohen?"

Mommy nodded. "I knew that, I guess, but I didn't think about it. Do you want to go by your U'tanse name?"

"Naw, I'm used to Barclay. Luke would be confused."

"Well, you have options. Maybe you'll get a title when you get older like your father did."

"The U'tanse people are excited to meet the first 'rejoined' U'tanse, whatever that means."

Daddy had been listening. He said, "That's right. Sammy, you're a very important person to the U'tanse. For centuries, nobody was ever sure if there ever was going to be a rejoined humanity."

. . .

The beam projector was nearly as large as the station itself. It was built during the last days before the Plague and never put into service. It was theoretically powerful enough to gradually move moons or planets, but it wasn't charged up beyond a starting level.

While a crew of Nuren, U'tanse and Uralites climbed through the interior, Ohen showed off some of the exterior features in the observation lounge with Sammy as his assistant. Various groups came by over the next few days, where they could get a look at the huge device.

A Hurf asked Sammy to focus on the rings at the edge of the beam projector. When the image zoomed in closer, they could see a group of four space-suited figures floating around same area.

Sammy said, "It's big."

The Hurf said, "Yes, I've never seen anything like it. It's amazing that humans have created beam projectors this large. Other species have tried and failed. It was always assumed that there was a physical limitation. When they tried, it always exploded."

"So this is a new thing?"

Another Hurf, but with an identical voice flickered its fur and said, "I hope so. We'll have to analyze the Nuren report, but Humans are too promising a race to leave on the black list. But like I say, we'll have to wait on the report."

Sammy was conscious of his father listening in on the conversation. Sometimes he got in trouble when talking to the adults, but the Hurf never seemed to mind talking to a kid like him. It was nice to be treated like a grown up.

. . .

Billie and her father, now going under the name George Linsey, were living alone together in Mexico City when the news was announced that Project-scale beam projectors were allowed as a keystone human invention, covering the license for the tractor/pressor beam technology itself.

"This is good, isn't it?" Billie asked.

"Perhaps. If humanity hadn't come up with something to tempt the Galactics, then they would have just gone away for hundreds of years, maybe thousands, and humans would have just had to make do like they have up until now.

"Perhaps it would have been better that way, to be left alone. But now, there's the possibility that humans will invent something that will allow them to purchase starships. That'll open up the wider universe to human exploration."

"Is that good?"

"I don't know. For me, I think it would be interesting to play the tourist and visit other star systems. Whether in a hundred years or even longer, I hope that much happens. I've been everywhere on Earth and it doesn't sound like Mars or Luna are much more than reworked versions of what we see here."

Billie sniffed. "Well I haven't seen enough of the world. I just play school girl with children bigger and dumber than I am, then pick up and move before I get to know any of them. I'd love to travel like a tourist and see the sights."

"We'll travel again soon."

She sighed. "Yes, just a little girl with Daddy at her side. I'd love to travel alone."

"Nobody would let you. You still look like you need someone to change your diapers."

"Don't you dare. I can take care of myself. Just nobody knows that."

"Be patient. You'll have a very long life to see everything you could possibly want to see."

She glared. "So you say."

The Haj Option

Ruel Johnson flicked his fingers at Sammy in the hallway. Sammy checked to see if anyone was watching and then scampered over to the maintenance office where Ruel was often working.

"What's up?"

Ruel closed the door. He gestured to the computer. "Event notification showed up for you. It's probably Luke again."

Sammy scooted into the chair and typed in his code. Shortly, there was giggle as he read Luke's tale of being recruited to monitor the visitors scouring the library, hunting for any book describing inventions. Luke was enjoying laying down the law when any of the adult researchers violated any of the library's strict rules regarding the preservation of those ancient books.

Supposedly every library in the solar system, including the great library on the Alexandria station, were being searched for something, anything, that humans had invented that wasn't already discovered by some over race and cataloged in the Galactic's records. There were a few things, but the total credits earned were far less than what was needed to buy even one starship core.

After Sammy typed in his tales of talking with the diplomats and Galactics, hoping to one-up Luke's bragging, he logged off with a sigh. It was rare that they managed to get computer time at the same time and have a real talk, although the speed-of-light delay caused some giggles on its own.

"Thanks Ruel."

"You're welcome. By the way, I think I have a message for your father. Could you let him know that his friend Haj would like to have a word with him?"

Sammy nodded, "Sure."

And then he was off. He'd been told that a Click was going to be helping with one of the technical evaluation sessions at the station's hub and he desperately wanted to sneak in to see it. In the time he'd been living at the station, he'd only seen a Click once, and that was through the display screen. He had to get up close to one. Luke could never top that.

. . .

Ohen frowned and asked, "Who told you this?"

Sammy shrugged, "Ruel. He's one of the maintenance workers in the station. He sometimes lets me have access time on his computer."

Ohen nodded. He'd ask questions about his son sneaking access to the station's computers some other time. If Haj left him this request for contact rather than just directly trying to contact him on Ohen's own computer, then it needed to be kept secret. The station had many advantages as a place to live and work, but there was really no assumption of secrecy. In spite of good materials, Ohen could hear voices from other living quarters. Not even textual messages via keyboard and display were totally safe from snooping. The flood of uncovered inventions from previous eras had brought many things to light that maybe should have stayed buried, including spying techniques used in earlier eras. Regardless of whether they could ever purchase a starship or not, humanity was experiencing a surge of technological advancement just because the strangers had arrived. Whether that would prove to be a good thing or not was yet to be determined.

But Haj wanted to talk, secretly, so that meant he had to take the boat out for a spin. It had been a long time.

Ohen contacted the station manager and requested port time. The excuse was to check the boat's systems prior to their return to Luna. So many other delegations had left that it wasn't an unusual request.

He had time between a couple of tech evaluation sessions so he took the boat out to ten light-seconds away from the station and the Galactic's starship. He had logged his course with Project Command, so he wasn't surprised to find a small cylindrical ship waiting silently at his destination. Ohen opened the outer airlock door.

Roman Al-Hajji, "call me Haj", came in through the airlock, without a spacesuit. Not that he needed one. He was carrying a briefcase and smiled.

"It's been a while, Ohen."

"Yes. I assumed you wanted to talk in secret." He waved at the cabin, isolated by the endless vacuum of space. "I guess this is as secret as I can manage."

Haj nodded. "This will do nicely. I've been wanting to talk with you about the negotiations with the Galactics. How is it going?"

Ohen shook his head sadly. "I've been living and breathing this for nearly two years now. At least we've got the TP technology license covered, but we've trotted out nearly every invention that's been created since the people began chipping stones for knives. The Galactics look it over, and then point to something in their catalog that is identical and was invented thousands of years ago by some other race. It's discouraging."

Haj nodded. Ohen was sure he had been monitoring every meeting. He was the computer system, after all. Originally named Hodgepodge by the ancestor of all the U'tanse, this computer system had been running itself since the time of the supernova flare well over a thousand years ago. The computer personality had only survived by keeping its existence secret and watching everything humanity did.

"I have a suggestion."

Ohen raised his eyebrows. "Oh? What is it?"

Haj smiled, and Ohen had to remind himself again that Haj was just an artificial body for that immense distributed computer system.

"I'd suggest that you offer me to the Galactics."

Ohen frowned. "They have computers. They've looked at our computers and didn't think they were anything different from what they already have."

Haj shook his head. "They are wrong. They just saw computers and assumed they knew what they were looking at. I have had enough time now to closely examine their computer technology and it is only slightly more advanced than the units the U'tanse created.

"You don't realize just how advanced my computers are. A human using one of my portable computers is only tapping into a tiny fraction of its true power. The rest of its capacity is used communicating with all the other computers, running my distributed intelligence. I market and sell the computer services that humans want, but I design and build the computers I need."

Ohen didn't comprehend what that hive mind was capable of doing, but he knew that at a minimum, it was monitoring every spaceflight in the system, as well as tracking every orbit of every planet, moon, asteroid or station. It encoded and routed every computer message and answered endless questions. It was the living heartbeat of the Solar system.

He also knew Project Command and Haj were secretive about what else was going on. The idea that there was an actual intelligence with its own personality running on top of all those computers was the biggest secret of all. Only two humans actually knew that it existed.

And only those two, Ohen and Gabriel, had seen the artificial human bodies that the intelligence occasionally occupied. There was Haj and Ohen suspected there were duplicates of him because sometimes Haj appeared in odd places when he was officially elsewhere. He also suspected John Lupin on Luna and what about this Ruel on the station? Unless the computer revealed itself, he'd never know. How many artificial bodies existed, distributed throughout human-occupied space? It was certainly dangerous for Hodgepodge to have too many, but knowing what humanity was doing was something the computer mind needed to be on top of.

Yes, this was some technology that the Galactics might value.

"Haj, I'm uncomfortable with this. Are you seriously suggesting that we sell you to the Galactics? Like a slave?"

Haj smiled. "I don't think you understand my viewpoint in this. A technological civilization is my habitat. I infected Earth's when it was weakened by the Betelgeuse supernova flare. I moved in, repaired and replaced it. I provided value by supplying all the computer and communication services that humanity ever needed.

"And now I can do the same elsewhere. It's just as if humans discovered a new habitable planet. This is potentially new living space for me. Nothing will change, I will hide my over-mind and just provide services to these new customers so that I may grow and expand. You humans want starships to expand into the galaxy. I want to do the same, and this is my way to do it."

Ohen thought about it. "Are you asking my permission for this? Because I am a descendant of Abe, your creator?"

Haj smiled again. "No. That era is past. I'm asking you, as a friend who is in a unique position to know the wider truth, to help me present this option to the Galactics. I have other methods available. This is just the smoothest path."

Ohen shrugged. "Okay, how exactly would this work?"

Haj opened his briefcase and opened a notebook that, page by page, explained it all. He'd done all the paperwork in advance.

. . .

Ohen stood before the group, there were humans, Hurf and Nuren present.

"I have a demonstration to make," he gestured at the computers on the table, "but before that I have a little history to present."

On the display was a timeline, marking major events in human history, starting with the supernova flare, and including the events of the Terraforming Project and the Plague.

"At approximately this point in our history, about at the genetic Die-Off after King Thomas's War, human computer technology took off and became ubiquitous. The messaging system that rode on top of its mesh-distributed network has provided the connectivity and computer power that was necessary for the terraforming project to exist.

"Behind the scenes, there was an organization, popularly called the Gnomes, that supplied the computers. Eventually it became so automated that it moved under the umbrella of the Project itself and dropped out of sight."

He changed the display. "What I'm about to show you has been running in asteroidal factories at the minimal level to keep the Project running, but it can be rapidly scaled up."

There was a large, flat station, covered in solar panels and access ports, floating in space.

"Each factory can be loaded with raw materials and it will autonomously fabricate a number of different computers. With the appropriate programming, one of these factories can even create a duplicate of itself. At this moment, dozens of new factories are being created to handle the demand for new computers, now that trade between the worlds of the Solar system has opened up."

He gestured at the table. "All these computers were created recently from a factory in orbit near Vesta. I'll now demonstrate the capabilities of these computers."

He went through a variety of demonstrations and called a Hurf up to give it commands in a variety of Galactic languages.

"These units have keyboards designed for human hands, but ones can be easily configured for other designs, including waterproof ones usable by the Kwish."

There were questions, including how the human computers were able to handle the translation issues without access to the Galactic's translation software.

The Nuren moved into the conversation when it was discovered the computational depth that these simple units were capable of handling. A second round of tests was planned. There were long discussions looking at the energy demands and what raw materials were needed for the factories.

It took over a month, but when all the Galactic races expressed a desire for these seed factories, it was acknowledged that this self-replicating computer technology was far superior to what the Galactics used. It was classified as a type-2 technology. Although each purchaser race could make more factories for themselves once they had the first one, the Solar system would be the only initial source of seed factories. Nobody else could sell it to any other race. Humanity held the license for them.

Initial negotiations showed that humanity should be able to purchase at least a few starships from the Click before long.

Ohen spent many long nights wondering to himself how many factories existed in secret places throughout the Solar system producing Haj's brothers or who knew what other devices Hodgepodge might desire.

. . .

Sammy looked at his parents. Baby Helen played with her toys on the floor, ignoring the announcement.

"So we're going back to Luna?"

His father nodded. "Yes, our job here is done. The Galactics will be leaving within a few months, after loading two of the computer factories in their cargo hold, but they don't need diplomats for that. Your grandfather has been pestering us to come back home for months now. Don't you want to go back to Stampz and be with your friends?"

Sammy nodded, still frowning. "Yes, I guess. It's just a change. How much time to I have?"

His mother smiled, "Do you have goodbyes to make?"

Sammy shrugged, "I guess." It had been two years out of his six, living here on the station. He'd almost forgotten about running in the fields and paying attention to the winds so he wouldn't be caught outdoors at the wrong time.

Yes, and maybe he needed to say goodbye to a few people as well. It was going to be such a change!

"I'll be the strongest boy my age, won't I?" They'd been sleeping at Mars gravity, but he ran all over the station, quite used to a full Earth gravity. He didn't even think about it anymore, once his muscles had adapted.

Ohen chuckled. "Yes, and Helen will be the strongest little girl, too."

Sammy nodded. "It's okay then." It was time to return to Luna.

Billie's Question

Billie rode her scooter into the storage shed at full speed, trusting her instincts to be able to bring it to a stop even before the automatic door managed to close. The home in Los Angeles was still three blocks away, but she couldn't show up at their house in these clothes.

She'd been pleased to find the row of coded sheds so close to home. Keyed to her personal code, not even Daddy could get in and check on what she was doing out of his sight. Her only worry was timing her entrances and exits to the swings of the security camera looking for thieves. If she got in and out quickly enough, there wouldn't even be a visual record of her arriving dressed like a short businesswoman and leaving looking like a teenager just out of school.

She had three sets of personal identity papers stashed in the shed. One for her schoolgirl identity, and two different adult personas. At her current physical development, she looked about twelve or thirteen, but could pass for a couple of years older in school. One adult was a thirty-year-old midget who had a part-time job in the back office of a construction firm, handling the accounting. The other identity was new, a persona named Beth she'd put together as a personal project. She'd even gotten the forged documents without her father's help.

She'd taken twenty-five year old Beth out for a spin a few times, even visiting a local bar this afternoon to test out her card. Sipping the beer was a personal achievement, but she didn't really like the taste. She didn't stay long when a couple of guys tried to chat with her.

Dressing as an adult took extra care to age her face appropriately. Clothes to pad out her body shape were easy enough to acquire, but people paid more attention to the details in her face when trying to judge her age.

But now, she had to wipe off her adult face and return home as the teenager her neighbors expected.

Daddy had it easy. According to him, his physical appearance had gradually stabilized at late-twenties. His various identities usually varied only ten years older than that, so it was easy for him to maintain the look. She'd seen him change from one persona to another by just tensing some muscles in his face and slumping over a bit.

She wondered again what his true age was. Big parts of his life were secrets that he didn't share with anyone. The last time she threw a tantrum and demanded to know more, he was firm. A secret shared is no secret at all, and he threw her teenage hormones and tantrums back at her as evidence she wasn't old enough to know everything yet.

Her true age was closer to the accountant she presented at work, but she didn't really count years anymore. Daddy always discouraged birthday celebrations, for good reason. An age was just a data point on a forged document, and it always would be.

She drove her scooter into the shed beside the house and wasn't surprised to find Daddy browsing another magazine with large picture spreads of alien worlds under distant suns. He was always dreaming of the day he could go play tourist.

Billie would be happy enough to travel around the local area. Daddy claimed they traveled enough every time they had to change identities, but none of that was really touristy stuff. They were always trying to avoid the crowds and trying to find a nice bland home to live in.

She didn't really want to give up her new identities simply to go see the mountains either. Just because Daddy had gone everywhere and seen everything didn't mean she was bored with it all like he was. A nice vacation was something she'd pestered him about for years but without any luck.

He glanced her way. "You're upset. School or work?"

She sighed and set her bag on the table. "Oh, nothing serious. Just boys being boys."

"School boys are much too young for you."

"I know that!" she snapped. None of her classmates were much beyond toddlers in her perspective.

"Not a teacher, I hope." There had been an incident two years before, when she was a different girl in a different city. The literature teacher began recommending increasingly adult stories to her and his private study sessions with his prized, mature student got uncomfortably close to the danger zone. Rather than make a scandal, it was just another excuse to update the birth certificate and move locations.

"No, I've learned that lesson. I'm quite stupid when appropriate."

"Somebody at work then?" he asked.

Billie just wished he'd drop it. "Why do you care? How many girlfriends have you brought home just in the last ten years? And not all of those were fake mothers for me either!"

He sighed. "I guess that's fair. Sooner or later you're going to be attracted to someone, I guess. It doesn't really matter. I mean they're not even the same species as us. You're not going to get pregnant and your immune system can shake off any diseases you might pick up."

It was hardly a birds and bees lecture, but usually Daddy just avoided the question. But he continued, "I just worry about your disguise. Once you start taking off clothes, none of your fake padding will help you. Your immature body shape will betray you and there will be questions. If you get into that kind of situation, then be sure to warn me, so I can make preparations to move."

Billie closed her eyes and tried to keep from blowing her top again. It never helped. "So you don't care if I find a lover as long as he's into little kids?"

He waved his hand. "No, I don't mean that. Honestly, I'd rather it was just you and me on a deserted piece of land where you could grow to maturity without all of these kinds of troubles. But the reality is that we're living in a human culture and we look human. We're both attractive people and now that your teenage hormones have started to kick in, we'll have to face these kinds of issues."

Her brain swirled with questions. What could she get away with asking this time?

"Daddy. You've never explained this. You always say that only the two of us are special. We're a slow-maturing human-like species. You say I can't even get pregnant with a regular guy. I know you're much older than me. Hundreds of years older. You're always telling me stories from different historical eras, and I know you're not just making it all up."

She raised a finger. "If I can't get pregnant, can you impregnate a human girl? I've never seen you worried about that."

He sighed. "No. It's impossible."

She spread her hands. "Then where did I come from? If you are the only other person of my species, and my birth mother was human, there's a contradiction."

He looked off at the front window. He was very good at reading her face, but she was good at it too. He was debating whether to tell more of his secrets.

He closed his eyes, and then turned to face her. "Have a seat. It's a long story."

She sat, her heart racing. Daddy's secrets were too important to miss a syllable.

He said, "Back in the time of King Thomas's War, the kingdom of Australia was making waves in the world economy with its genetic engineering."

This was all old news. She'd been taught this stuff at school time after time. Her only struggle was keeping quiet and avoiding correcting her teachers when they made errors.

She nodded. "All the genetically altered people died. The Die-Off."

"Technically, correct." He nodded. "However, there were a different class of genetic products. Instead of taking a base genetic code and patching changes into it, they were also experimenting with creating a whole genome from scratch by reading the desired traits out of a database. That's how the merpeople were created. The military on Australia wanted a undersea soldier and rather than patch normal people with gills, they created a whole new species. And even when all the gene patches failed during the war—probably due to some genetic disease that targeted those patches—the merpeople were never affected."

Billie was already putting together the pieces, but she bit her tongue. She wanted him to say the words.

He nodded, "So some secret laboratory had a bright idea. They already had all human genetics recorded in their databases. I'm not entirely sure what their original goal was, probably radiation resistance or something like that. But they didn't stop there.

"With the whole of human genetics available to them, they decided to make the best human possible. They chose the best metabolism, the best immune system, the best intelligence, and importantly, they didn't include natural aging. They created a genetic code from start to finish. There were some alterations, the slow maturity is one of them. They also changed several things like reduced cartilage growth so an old person wouldn't have excessively large noses and ears. They tried hard to make their perfect person.

"And then they created a couple of prototypes, one male named 'Alpha' in their records and one female, named 'Beta'.'"

Her heart was racing. "You were Alpha?"

He nodded.

"And Beta?"

He spread his hands. "The war ended with the Die-Off. Vast numbers of people who had genetic work done to improve themselves or to cure diseases died of a horrific decaying process, trapped in concentration camps because the remaining population was so frightened of everything tainted with the genetic label. Any laboratory that worked in that field was destroyed and the scientists were often hounded to death. That whole field of science was banned."

"But … Beta? What happened?"

"The laboratory that created Alpha and Beta turned those infants loose. Maybe they were afraid to be caught with them in their possession, scared for their own safety. The scientists went into hiding on a space colony. Two helpless infants were left behind, on their own in a world where they would be killed if they were discovered to be different."

He shrugged. "I survived, going from one foster parent to another. I was smart and when I puzzled out the nature of my ailment, I learned how to change my name and pretend to be a different age. I assume Beta had to survive on her own just like I did.

"Only when I was much older did I track down a few records from that laboratory and discovered that she existed. I hunted for Beta, but I never saw her before she was killed during the Plague."

Billie gasped. "So I'm not Beta."

He smiled. "Not exactly. In a dark crevasse on Ceres, I found the frozen and damaged body of Beta. I extracted her genetic code and created an embryo. After that, I needed a host mother to bring you to term. You were never her actual daughter, but she didn't understand that."

He stretched back. "The rest, you know. There was a series of foster mothers. Each lasted until she worried too much about your slow growth."

Billie's mind was tangled with questions. Some she didn't know how to express.

"Beta died hundreds of years ago, during the Plague?"

"Yes, she was trapped on one of the destroyed space habitats. She was brilliant. She almost rescued herself from an impossible situation."

"When did you find her?"

"Just recently, when the barrier to space was lifted. I had been trapped on Earth all that time."

"But you knew when she died?"

He tensed up. "I saw the flash when the impact on Ceres happened. We had just exchanged a few messages and I was trying to rescue her. I had just then discovered that Beta was real and had survived as I had."

Billie saw something in his eyes that she'd never seen before. "What happened then?"

He shook his head and looked at the ceiling. "Disassociation. You know how I can immerse myself in my various personas? Well, I lost myself for a long, long time. I forgot who I was."

"You said you recovered Beta's genetic code? By yourself? Does anyone else know?"

He told her about the Chilean base with the scavenged Australian machines.

"The scientists who created Alpha and Beta escaped to space?"

His expression changed, hard and dark. "They didn't survive, not a single one of them. I made sure of it."

Billie had decades of experience with him. There were times when she just needed to change the subject quickly and think about things later. This was one of them.

"What do you know about Beta's life?"

"Not much. I'd just discovered her when the disaster happened. She was a medical doctor. One of the first ones to discover the Plague and then, she was unfortunate enough to be on a doomed habitat." He smiled. "She must have been someone special."

He looked at Billie. "Are you okay? Too much data?"

She shook her head. "No, but there's a lot I need to think about. I may have other questions later."

He nodded and went back to his magazines. He said he had an evening meeting with a customer.

Billie turned her back on him and headed to her room.

She had a lot to think about, but out of his sight. She didn't want him to read her expression. Building like a storm wave on the ocean was the idea that Daddy, her father, was never that. He just might be a monster.

The Devil's Daughter

Billie sat in her room and fumed. *At work, I'm an adult. I am an adult, this teenage body is just a curse, a medical condition.*

But her bedroom was decorated like any teenaged girl's place. Perhaps it was a little bare, since she didn't have as many keepsakes. Changing locations frequently meant a lot of things had to be left behind.

She sat in her desk chair and waited, all her fury playing out inside her skull, with a healthy dose of raging hormones. But she had years worth of training to keep her from acting out when it was important to appear calm. And it was very important now.

At the time she predicted, a Christmas ornament on her shelf blinked on for a few seconds. Years earlier, she'd stuck a tracking decal on Daddy's vehicle. She'd been through a few of them, and he'd never indicated that he'd noticed. Sometimes she needed a quick alert when he left the house and when he returned. When your father is the smartest person in the world, sometimes it took a little extra effort to get some privacy.

Not that he was really her father. That had been a lie. He was model A and she was model B. No, she was a clone of model B. She only had his word that she was an identical copy at that.

History and now his own words confirmed that genetic technology was lost, and yet he still had access to it. He was smart enough to use that forbidden technology to bring a dead person back for a second try. And so much of what he'd told her today matched up with what she already knew about him.

He liked the merfolk, even though everyone else considered them a great pest. Every year, she'd hear about somebody proposing to wipe them out, although nobody knew how to accomplish that. Direct military attacks would require a navy, and the merpeople were very good at sinking ships. You couldn't poison the ocean without wiping out humanity as well. Perhaps a targeted genetic disease would work, but nobody had that technology anymore.

Nobody but... the man acting as her father.

A few more pieces of the puzzle came together. She was horrified, but not really shocked, when he'd said that he had wiped out the scientists who had created them. She always knew he was capable of achieving his ends with efficient and evil means. She'd watched time after time as he'd left former lovers, either calmly walking away or leaving them suffering through the illusion that he and their daughter had been killed.

And now he'd calmly admitted that he had killed people, perhaps a large number of people. He'd stated it with such satisfaction.

Daddy was a homicidal sociopath.

Is that a family trait? Am I that way as well? She'd certainly lived a life of deception. She had no real friends, only friendly acquaintances that she could drop out of her life at a moment's notice if she needed to run. She lied several times a day as she swapped her identities and took on different personas for different parts of her life.

She always told herself it was necessary. For as long as she had to be both child and an adult, there would be this need to lie.

And she was also lying to Daddy, hiding her true self from him. How long had she been aware that he was dangerous?

Today's questions had been probes, trying to get a feel for what he really thought about her and boys. He'd seemed callous about the idea. He seemed okay with the idea that she might have a sexual relationship with someone, but the underlying message was that any boy she might get close to was a danger to them, someone to be abandoned in a flash.

But now that she knew he wouldn't stop at murder, would any boy be really safe getting that close to her? What was Daddy really capable of doing if he felt threatened?

Billie pulled a stuffed animal off her shelf. It looked worn from years of use.

"Wolfie? I'm scared of Daddy."

The stuffed animal's eyes turned on and it said, "What did he do this time?"

"It's not what he's done, it's what I'm afraid he might do."

The little personal diary built into the toy wolf had been a simple device, originally, but Billie had probed at its limits and found a way to reprogram it. For years, it had become her only confidant, hiding her words encrypted behind her personal code, responsive to her voice only.

She told Wolfie a summary of the talk, and her conclusion that Daddy wasn't who he'd always claimed to be and that he was indeed a dangerous murderer.

The childlike voice replied, "But doesn't the fact that he's revealed this to you prove that he trusts you?"

"I don't know. I'm not really his daughter and that throws everything up in the air. I could always trust that link with him before, but it's not there anymore."

"What is your link with him now?"

She closed her eyes and hugged her toy wolf. It was urgent that she solve this dilemma as quickly as possible, and before he returned home from his business meeting and she had to play her dutiful daughter role again.

"I'm a second try at Beta." She reviewed what he'd said about the original. She could still see the look on his face as he'd talked about how brilliant this woman was, even through he'd never actually met her. "He liked Beta and was enraptured by her. She was just like him, just as brilliant, just as immortal, the only woman of his species."

Billie shook. It was as plain as day.

"Wolfie, I'm not really his daughter. He's growing me to maturity so that I can be his mate."

She flashed back over the previous incident with the teacher who was becoming too physical with her. How had Daddy reacted to that?

She knew how the public reacted when an adult seduced a child—there was a general revulsion at the idea. Daddy never showed that reaction, he reacted as to any other threat of discovery and changed their identities.

Maybe he wasn't disgusted with the idea of a much younger lover. It was what he was planning for himself from the beginning. It was just that he was taking the long view, growing her to maturity. He'd taken other lovers who were younger in calendar age than she was. This was normal to him.

"Wolfie, does the fact that I've told Daddy that I'm interested in boys change our relationship? Will he start acting like I'm a potential lover, instead of a daughter? He's never had any difficulty seducing a new girl when we move to a new town. He's had centuries of experience at it. Will he start focusing on me now?"

The toy said, "Your voice shows fear."

"What should I do?"

"The general fear response is fight or flight."

Billie's eyes were wet with tears. "Fight or flight? That's impossible either way."

She was horribly outmatched. Physically, she had no fighting skills beyond some rudimentary martial arts classes several lives back. Daddy was never intimidated by any threat he'd come across, and she suspected that even without weapons, he could kill or maim anyone.

But was flight possible?

"Wolfie, am I as smart as Daddy?"

"I don't know."

She nodded to herself. According to the tale, Alpha and Beta were both infants when they were abandoned. Probably they were a pair, male and female prototypes with identical genetics except for superficial coloring and the fact that they were different genders. So the basics, like intelligence, were probably the same.

Daddy had more experience than her, by centuries, but the problem of hunting for one person among millions of others was still a big task.

She needed money, a head start, and a distraction.

. . .

Barry Childers, Alpha's current name, really didn't have any objection to going to work on a daily basis. He was just killing time until Billie matured enough to pass for an adult consistently. He didn't really need the money, since he'd been investing for a long time now. Changing personas and moving every few years allowed him to dabble in various careers as well. It was a game.

This time he was an agent, selling aircraft to various companies. It was an exciting time in the industry. The new and expensive TP-powered craft were arriving from the revitalized space cities, taking the high end of the market, while the still air-worthy alcohol-powered craft were finding their new value in the used market.

He was climbing up the sales rankings, his long experience giving him the edge in selling expensive items to rich people and companies alike. He also had his eye on a few craft that might be handy to own himself. When he had to vanish, arranging untraceable transportation was always an issue. Having a small, but modern TP craft stashed in a remote garage would be a valuable asset. The ones he'd left in storage hundreds of years ago were gone, discovered or destroyed.

There was just the details of moving money from one of his accounts to another fake company name to make the new purchase. He'd need to do that sometime in the next few months.

He parked at his house and went in, half expecting another discussion with Billie. He'd been a little reluctant to reveal her origins until she was a little older, ideally when she was physically mature enough to fixate on him as her ideal mate. Still, she was an adult in everything but appearance and teenage hormones and she would need the real truth before she fell in love with some inappropriate human.

"Billie?" he called out.

From her room, her voice replied, "I'm busy now!"

He frowned, but she was leading two lives, school and work, and probably had homework to deal with. But, she needed her sleep and it was already getting late. He'd just talk with her in the morning. Maybe he'd fix breakfast, rather than letting her raid the pantry on her own as had been their latest habit.

He went on to bed, but didn't immediately fall asleep. Something was wrong, but he couldn't quite identify it. He reviewed the day.

The conversation with Billie was the most important, but he was thorough, also reviewing what he'd read in the magazine and the three potential sales he had in process at his work. Nothing jumped out at him.

There was only one thing he could follow up on before tomorrow's work day. He got up and went to Billie's bedroom door. Opening it without an invitation had been a major battle three years earlier in another city. But, there was light leaking from under the door.

He listened carefully, but there was no sound of activity. Under ideal conditions, he should even be able to hear her breathing, but the sounds of the city were constant and had to be ignored.

"Billie?"

"I'm busy now!"

He blinked. That didn't sound right. It was identical to what he'd heard earlier, and there was still no sounds of activity inside.

The door was locked, but no lock stopped him for more than a few seconds. He opened it, to see her lit room, but Billie wasn't there.

He stood motionless at the entrance, carefully looking at everything. Nothing much looked out of place. The room was lived in, and while Billie kept things tidy, it was hardly spotless.

"Billie?"

The toy wolf, which she had brought with her through at least five moves, spoke, "I'm busy now!" The eyes had lit up for just an instant.

His memories flashed back to when it was new. There's been a sound maker feature that made cute wolf-cub noises, but nothing like a voice recorder was advertised.

He took three steps and plucked it from the shelf. He could feel the hard shape under the padding. He didn't bother to investigate further. If he could reprogram a gadget like that, then likely Billie could too.

A single sheet of paper was isolated on her desk. He turned it over.

"Daddy, if you're reading this, then you noticed I'm not home tonight. I got an invitation from a friend at school just after you left and decided to take her up on the sleep over. I'm not telling you her name because you'd call her parents or spy on us and it would be embarrassing. That's a deadly handicap in schoolgirl social circles, so just don't do it. I'll be back after work tomorrow. You know I can handle myself. I've been doing it for years."

He read it twice more, looking for clues to deception, but he'd trained her himself and he couldn't trust the superficially honest words.

His biggest question was whether it really was a schoolgirl she'd gone to sleep with, or some guy. That had been the focus of her questions. She had never really answered his question about the "boys being boys" that had triggered the whole conversation.

He hurried to the computer in the study room. Some time back, he'd put a tracking decal on her scooter, up under the seat where it wouldn't be discovered. Soon he had a map displaying its location. Cross-referencing the address with the list of students that he'd acquired out of habit when they moved to the city, he frowned when there was no match.

It wasn't a student's house. So the schoolgirl sleep over was a lie. Likely it was a coworker. That was so dangerous! He'd spelled it out for her. Padded clothes only worked when they were worn!

He was furious. If they had to move abruptly, it would mess up his plans to acquire an aircraft for his own; not to mention that he'd been enjoying this job.

Should he race the three miles to interrupt their date? What would be the side effects of that? Nobody at her work knew about him. She was supposedly an adult who lived alone. His appearance would destroy that job and that persona. She could never use it again. It'd also be a scandal that people would talk about for some time. Abandoning a life should be done as quietly as possible. An old persona should be easily forgotten by everyone.

He reused a few valuable identities, but only after a few decades had passed and there was no chance of old acquaintances discovering him in his new location, not having aged a bit.

But what if he tracked her scooter down anyway, and just stayed nearby in case she realized she'd gotten in over her head and needed rescue.

He nodded to himself. That was best. And besides, he could find out more about this new lover of hers. Sometimes it was possible to preserve a compromised persona by removing the person who had uncovered a dangerous secret.

He checked the fuel level before starting out, just in case something happened that required a long drive. He carried the computer with him, wishing for the old days when every vehicle had its own computer and could display maps. That day would return soon enough, now that the space cities were churning out computers in vast numbers.

No sooner had he arrived at the marked location on the tracker than he realized something was wrong. This wasn't a residence, it was a shopping area, and it was well past midnight.

He checked the tracking map again. The location had moved. A minute later, it had moved again. She was going somewhere. While grateful she wasn't in someone's bed, he worried at what she might be doing at this late hour.

Following the dot on the map, he soon pulled to within a block of it. There was a little traffic, but there was no scooter in sight.

The dot moved and so did he. Shortly he pulled past it and winced when he saw the tracking decal down low on the side of a police patrol. He turned away and pulled into the nearest vacant parking lot.

Billie had found the tracking dot and put it on a decoy. Could she be running away from home?

It hadn't looked like her room had been scavenged for clothes and she'd left her favorite stuffed animal behind.

But there was one thing he could check right now. Using the computer he checked the bank account jointly shared by him and schoolgirl Billie. The money had been drained. It had been transferred less than an hour after he had left home for his business meeting.

He knew she had a separate account where her job salary was deposited and he'd never tried to spy on that. That she would try to run away was unthinkable. They'd been close partners for many years now. They trusted each other.

But it was undeniable. Something had upset her and she was evading him.

He frowned. She'd find it a lot harder to escape than she thought!

Hunting Billie

The nighttime was working against him. He could only chase her down if he knew where she was, and sadly, his sources of information were asleep. He looped through her parts of the city, checking the school parking lot and where she worked.

Billie wasn't stupid enough to leave her scooter out in plain sight, especially after she went to the trouble to move the tracking decal to another vehicle, but he couldn't afford to skip the simple checks.

Then he went home and systematically checked every potential hiding place in her room. When he gutted Wolfie and examined the electronics, he had to admit that it was just a simple audio-only computer, with all the encryption that implied, rather than some cobbled together recorder which might scavenged for more detail.

Her closet and cabinets were still full of her clothes. Her travel bags were still in the closet, gathering dust from their last move. The only thing missing was her school bag. She'd packed very lightly.

He was aware that she changed clothes as she shifted from her school and work identities somewhere but he hadn't tracked that down when he had the chance. He doubted it would be worth the effort. He'd trained her well and probably she had some concealed or coded hideaway. Was that why she hadn't packed her school girl clothes? Was she going to travel as an adult, using the clothes she'd stashed elsewhere?

He attempted sleep. He could go days at a time without rest, but he might need those reserves later in the chase. Still, his mind was racing. His body got some rest, but he was still awake when his computer popped up with a notice from the school. Billie had missed her first-period class.

He calmed his mind and called the school.

"I'm sorry I didn't call the office earlier, but it's been hectic after Billie's accident."

"Oh my! What happened?"

"Just a little traffic accident, but I'm afraid Billie will be in the hospital for a while. Is there any classwork that I need to pick up for her? I guess I need to talk to her teachers and maybe get a list of any classmates that might want to know what happened to her."

He rambled on, gradually getting more information than the school secretary normally gave out. The only critical items were that none of the other students and none of the teachers had gone missing. There was always the possibility that Billie had planned an escape with a friend or lover.

No other missing people meant she was probably traveling alone, although he'd have to interrogate people from her workplace as soon as possible. A traveling companion would have been helpful. Billie had been trained to cover her tracks all her life, but it might be harder for her to protect an ordinary person with her.

After the school call, he contacted the police to report her scooter as stolen. Normally, he'd never get the police involved unless he owned them. Several times in his life, he'd collected an extensive network of people who would do anything he asked, but changing identities so often didn't make it worthwhile. In the last thirty years, they'd moved every two or three years, sometimes more frequently than that, although one rural community where they'd lived had so little curiosity about them that they lasted nearly four years before things became uncomfortable.

It was a little difficult to go to work and pretend everything was normal, but he couldn't claim family problems without making people curious. He had to find Billie soon, but without causing anyone to investigate him. He placed his order for one of the low-capacity TP aircraft for one of his fake identities, with a bonus for quick delivery. It was much more than an ordinary salesman could afford, but finding Billie was the most important thing in his life and he had to have maximum mobility. He could rebuild his cash reserves later.

...

Hank Burleson, the manager of the construction company where Billie worked was a little bemused by the aircraft salesman that had arrived at his door, pushing the idea of buying a used hover-rated craft to survey his worksites.

"No, Mr. Childers, I don't think that's something we could afford—although it sounds like fun."

"Why don't I take you to lunch and show you what we have in the catalog, just for browsing? It won't cost you a penny and it'll make me happy showing off all the great deals in fuel-based craft that have come on the market recently. Do you like steak?"

Hank had to take care of a few things first, but he admitted he could be tempted by a meal. That gave Barry a few minutes alone in the office to confirm that there weren't any likely travel companions missing. The company hadn't even noticed Billie was gone since she only arrived mid-afternoon for her shift.

After they ate, and after Hank toyed with the idea of a shuttle of his own, but just promised to think about it, Barry gave him a big salesman smile and hurried off.

He'd just gotten notification from a surveillance broker that claimed parking lot video of the bus and airports in the area. He'd have to do the facial recognition scanning himself because he couldn't supply photos of Billie in any of her various identities. He'd have to come up with software to match her body size and other details.

Frustrated, he made a voice call, hoping she would answer, but there was no response. He left a message. "Billie, please come home. We can talk about anything."

When there was no response to that, he considered the possibility that she didn't have a computer.

It didn't seem likely. The costs had gone down over the past few years as imports from space had increased, and they were too valuable to be without when on the run.

Billie just didn't want to talk to him. Maybe she thought it would give him clues as to her location, and it would. Voice calls would be best, because he could hear background noises, but even text replies could give him hints by their timing. If she was riding her scooter, then she would have to come to a stop somewhere to answer.

When he arrived at his office, Jonah Lawson, the owner called him into his office.

"What's this rush order? We've already committed that unit to Segfield Transportation."

Barry shrugged with a slight smile. "I'm familiar with Wavolish, and when they call, I have to jump. Besides, I was able to negotiate a nice bonus for fast delivery. I've even committed to making the delivery myself once it arrives at the staging port."

"Who is this Wavolish? I've never heard of them."

Barry shook his head. "Jonah, you've impressed me as running a respectable, honest operation here. Believe me when I say that you don't want to know anything about Wavolish. Just leave this whole deal up to me. Log your percentage and forget it ever happened."

The businessman frowned. "This doesn't sit right with me. And you're going to fly the thing itself? I saw that you claimed TP pilot certification when you came to work here, but you've never flown a thing since then."

The salesman shrugged with a sheepish smile, "Well, I'd have to dig for my paperwork, but I've logged quite a few hours in the air. I'd rather let someone else fly it to Wavolish, but I really don't want to get anyone else involved in this. It's something I can do, so I will."

His fake company's location was officially located in Africa and he really hoped Jonah would believe him and just let him handle everything without insisting on looking at the details.

"Well, okay. But I insist you write up the apology to Segfield Transportation for the delay!"

. . .

Barry was up hours with images flickering on the display, images of short females carrying their bags, waiting for buses or flights. Since Billie could easily disguise herself in many ways, he allowed the computer a lot of flexibility, which meant more possibilities for his own eyes.

He wasn't even confident that she was leaving the city. She might easily decide to hide out locally until he gave up his search before moving on.

He took breaks and made calls. His new aircraft was scheduled to arrive tomorrow at the Skylinks landing pads in Long Beach aboard one of the larger ground-to-space cargo craft. It would take time for the crew to unload just that one item among all the other product containers from the L4 factories. It would take quite a bit of cash to rearrange the ground-crew's schedule to get his item out early, and clear all the paperwork delays. He had the cash. Wavolish paid the freight.

A long life had taught him patience. As urgent as it was to get Billie back home and to resolve whatever conflict had triggered her into action, he knew that the only way to track her down was to follow all the possible leads and keep at it for as long as it took. Success was taking each step, not necessarily finding new clues. He'd pursued projects for years at a time without any measurable progress. A single day of frantic activity without any sign of her wasn't something to discourage him.

As time-consuming as the image search was, he'd need to get fresh raw images each day and process them, just to make sure she wasn't making her escape. The computer was learning which images he discarded immediately and which demanded a second look, so there should be fewer false positives over time.

He also had to review the cover story. He'd gotten very good at spinning and keeping consistent lies, but it was always better to have a complete tale outlined.

So he reviewed what he'd already told people and put them all together into a coherent tale.

Billie had swerved in traffic to miss a truck and skidded across the pavement, leaving her with face and body scrapes severe enough that he'd taken her to specialized medical care to try to prevent scarring. Her scooter had been taken by someone unknown, and thus the stolen vehicle report to the police.

But if anyone at the school asked, Billie didn't want visitors, now that she was bandaged and in treatment for her injuries. If anyone saw Billie, in contradiction to his tale, then it would be hard to prove because they had always taken care to limit photos.

But even if that happened, then they could always skip town like so many times before.

Billie's adult life was completely different, and he had no cover story for her going missing. Perhaps she would mail a note to her boss explaining an emergency, but he'd wait a few days for that. Adult Billie, she'd used the name Bobbie Smith, had no connection to Barry Childers and the address he'd found in her office records was a commercial postal box that couldn't be traced.

He made another message to Billie, under the assumption that even if she wasn't replying, she was still monitoring her messages. She had to log in regularly to access her bank account, if nothing else.

He gave her a summary of the cover story. If she knew she could return with no big scandal, that should make it easier for her. He didn't want her to think that she'd burned all her bridges and that it was impossible to return.

There was still no reply. He reviewed his schedule. He'd have to go to Skylinks in order to pick up his craft as soon as it was released.

He looked at the clock. Sleep now or never.

. . .

The chime from the computer brought him instantly awake. He tapped the keyboard to answer the voice call.

"Hello, this is Patrolman Wilson of the Coastal Guard. Is this Mr. Childers?"

"Yes. Do you have any information about my scooter?"

"Yes, we've found it. It looks like it was abandoned and hidden in trees near the highway." He gave map details. Barry promised to come there quickly to pick it up.

The scooter was halfway down the coast toward San Diego. Getting there and back to Long Beach in time to pick up the aircraft would be tight. But he had to get all the details possible, both from examining the scooter and anything the patrolman might have noticed.

Traffic was heavier than he expected, and it was obvious why Billie had taken that route. The road hugged the coastline and he remembered all the times she'd asked for a vacation to see the scenery. He'd usually turned her down. He had plans to take her all over the world and see everything, once she matured and they could tour as a couple, but he never told her that.

Was this escape just a reaction to that, wanting to see the world and giving up on his caution? Maybe her time as adult Bobbie Smith had made her impatient living as teenage Billie. He just didn't know, and it was critical to find her so they could talk and work this all out.

Patrolman Wilson was busy with a grocery store robbery, so Barry had to be content with reading the report and checking the scooter himself. It had been almost out of fuel, so he assumed she abandoned it rather than refueling for some reason. Checking the map found a bus station in easy walking distance from where the scooter had been hidden. She had decided to change travel modes—probably a good idea since she could disguise herself easier than she could change the look of the scooter.

Barry filled out the necessary paperwork and folded the scooter up into the cargo hold of his vehicle.

He called her. Again, no voice response. He left a message.

"Billie, I've recovered your scooter. It's still in good shape. I'll have it ready for you when you come home."

He had mixed feelings about letting her use the scooter again after having just tried to escape, but that scooter had been one of her favorite things, letting her travel freely without relying on him to ferry her places. They'd carried it through two moves, and he was glad he'd never registered it to any of their previous identities. Now, however, it was in the police database. Once she came back, he'd need to talk her into trading it for a new one.

He wished there was a way to embed a tracker under her skin in a way that she wouldn't be able to detect it. He'd worried about that centuries ago when he was young and he was afraid someone was hunting for him. Eventually he convinced himself that there was nothing like that in him. It was just that, when you're unique, it's easy to be paranoid, thinking there was someone behind the scenes trying to track you down.

Driving past the rural bus stop, he frowned. There was no sign of a security camera. She could have taken a bus back to Los Angeles, but it was much more likely that she'd continued on to the capital.

San Diego was a significant transportation hub. Rail lines went all over North America from there. There was a large airport as well as a dock with ships that had merfolk permits to travel to all parts of Asia.

He'd barely considered where she might be headed when his computer chimed a reply. It was text from Billie.

"Leave me alone! I'm never coming back!!! You can burn the scooter for all I care. I've never been your daughter and I'm never going to be your—"

It looked like the message had been chopped off, but there was no followup. He sighed. She was erratic. It was teenage hormones. It had to be.

. . .

Billie's hands were shaking and she forced herself to calm down. She should never have attempted the reply. It was just so frustrating that he'd found the scooter so fast. It was a mistake to have hidden it in the trees. She should have pushed it into the ocean or something. He was sure to follow her to San Diego now.

"Hey. Jerry! Mom said it's time to go."

She forced a smile and waved at her temporary brother, George. She'd been lucky to have discovered the mother and son and she was very grateful Mrs. Cole had bought her story that she was running away from an abusive father. With a little makeup, she was George's younger brother, at least through the entrance gates.

Billie's Escape

Barry raced north, heading to pick up his aircraft, fighting the urge to go south and track her down before she found refuge in San Diego. When he arrived at the Skylinks facility, he was supposed to play the role of an impatient businessman and it was very easy to do, yelling when the unloading was delayed. He was enraged when the initial checkout showed that the aircraft was shipped with a nearly drained power cell. He had to make arrangements to move it over to the public power center where large power cells shipped down from space had their load converted into electricity for the power grid.

He was able to arrange a high-speed direct transfer to get his craft powered up. Only then could he get authorization to fly it away. On the tarmac, he lowered the cargo ramp and drove his vehicle inside and secured it to the tie-down anchors. Then he logged the aircraft as the Vermillion and got permission to lift off. San Diego was his destination, at least for the first leg of the trip.

Once he was in the air and clear of the other aircraft, he started taking care of business. He contracted for surveillance video from all the major transportation centers in San Diego. He hand wrote an apology letter in Billie's handwriting to Bobbie Smith's boss, explaining a family emergency and sent a photo of it to a service that would send it as courier mail to her company. He made sure there was no follow up from Billie's school and researched a San Francisco medical center that had expertise in skin injuries, just in case he'd need to add details to the cover story.

In San Diego, he arranged hangar space for the Vermillion and drove around the city to see how much it had changed since the last time he'd been there, over a hundred years earlier. There was no sense in finding an apartment, he could easily live in the Vermillion for now.

. . .

Billie was almost the last person off the plane. Her face and body disguised as an elderly woman, she hobbled on a borrowed cane with a concerned flight attendant assisting to make sure she didn't fall. The Cole family were long gone, having been anxious to start their holiday in Hawaii.

"Thank you so much for your help," elderly Billie whispered, handing a crumpled bill to the lady. She adjusted her wide-brimmed hat and hobbled out into the crowded airport.

By the time she'd recovered her bag and visited the restroom to shed a few decades from her face, she was ready to face her new future, hopefully out from under the cloud of her "father".

. . .

The Vermillion was a low-end version of the aircraft being produced for atmospheric use on the habitable planets, a tractor/pressor powered craft that lacked airlocks and concentrated on aerodynamic shape and easy access ground hatches. Barry had chosen one with more cargo capacity and fewer passenger seats, but inside, it still had many of the features of the interplanetary craft used by the space cities. It was quite comfortable to live in, even quietly sitting in a hangar on the ground.

Barry used the large display screen for his surveillance videos. The San Diego feed was much harder to work through than the Los Angeles one had been. There were a lot more people visiting the capital or making their connections for other parts of the world. He had requested the feed beginning with the time Billie had hidden her scooter, so he was in catch-up mode.

After a few hours, he shook his head and decided to take a break. He walked down into the cargo level and pulled a seafood dish that he'd picked up when he was getting fresh eyes on the airport. Barry had long realized that even though he might be an ideal version of a human, he was still subject to fatigue and hunger just like everyone else.

As he was eating, he just put the raw feed of the airport lobby up with no pre-filtering, just to watch people moving around. After he was finishing off his meal, he noticed something. He backed the feed up by ten minutes and played it again.

There! The family of three. He remembered that the younger boy had shown up in the filtered feed, but he'd skipped over it. This time, there was something about the way he moved.

He watched as they gathered their bags and he shook his head. It wasn't Billie's bag, but she could have easily bought a replacement. The boys' clothes looked very similar. If that was Billie, could she have borrowed the older boy's shirt? It didn't quite fit right.

He skipped through the feed, following the three to a trans-pacific flight, with a stopover in Hawaii.

The rancher novel! Billie had read and fallen in love with the story of a traveler who had landed on Hawaii and during his struggles becoming a rancher, fell in love with the scenic island. Billie had urged him to vacation on Hawaii and he'd promised to consider it as their next home when they had to move.

But that was years ago. Had it made that much of an impression on her that she was trying to relive the novel?

He needed to confirm that she'd gone to Hawaii, and luckily the security videos for the Hawaiian airports were accessible. That particular flight stopped at Hilo airport on the big island for two hours before heading on to Jaixing in China.

Since he only had a few people to check, it didn't take long. The family was only two, the mother and the older boy, when they disembarked. He was almost ready to entertain the idea that she was heading on to China when he saw her in an elderly disguise. He even was able to see her after she changed her age, and she had definitely left the airport by the time the flight took off.

He felt relieved. The population of the Hawaiian Islands was much less than Los Angeles or San Diego. It would be easier to track her down there.

But it wouldn't be wise to warn her until he was much closer. She probably still had money enough to catch a quick flight elsewhere if she knew he was approaching.

. . .

Billie chose to be twenty, an age old enough to pass as an adult, but without having to use too much makeup. She was already regretting it. She'd never had as many rejections in her life.

Every job interviewer she'd approached had a quick dismissal for her. Simple labor like restaurant work expected younger people, some as young as ten. She couldn't attempt accounting work without forging some previous work experience that wasn't believable at her claimed age.

She'd have to move along the coast and hope to find someone more desperate for a worker. Billie was resolved to give it a month or so before moving on to a new location. Things weren't working out as well as she'd expected. Perhaps she needed to be older and approach her job hunting more slowly, as she had in Los Angeles. Her problem was limited money.

She had enough for a few months on the run, but unless she found a way to supplement her account, she might have to resort to begging or living off the land. She really didn't want to try her hand at theft. Getting herself added to the law enforcement databases would just wave a red flag at her "father". She was sure he already had some way of checking those.

Her computer chimed, and every muscle in her body tensed. It couldn't be good.

She forced herself to look at the message. The text scrolled on the display.

"Billie, I see you're looking for a job here in Hilo. Bad news I'm afraid. That novel you read was written over a hundred years ago and the culture here in the islands has become more restrictive since then.

"Nobody is going to hire you unless your family has lived here for generations. There are locals and outsiders, and no matter what the excuses you've been getting, the real reason is simple. You look like an outsider and nobody wants you around.

"I have my own transportation here, so you won't have to fly commercially. I'm even willing to live here for a while if you want to see all the island scenery for a while. I realize I haven't been very flexible about your desire to see more of the world and I can certainly change.

"But, we need to get back together and work through your complaints face to face. I haven't located where you're staying, but really, it won't be long. There's no reason for us to fight about this. We're family."

Billie's face was red with fury and frustration. He was in Hilo! He'd tracked her down and there was no way he'd let her get on another plane. He probably had tracking cameras everywhere by now. There was no one she could get help from. From the official records, all faked, she was just a runaway daughter. The truth wouldn't help. It would just label her as a monster as well.

She couldn't even go to sleep. If she did, there was every chance he'd locate her, bypass her locks and she'd wake up in his control after being drugged. Billie had seen him do that before with one of his girlfriends when she was causing troubles.

He'd be sweet and reasonable and in a few days he'd convince her that she'd been erratic and had just made a mistake about everything.

Daddy had been brainwashing people for centuries. He was very good at it. Billie wasn't at all sure she could resist. He'd watched her grow up, after all. He knew every book she'd read and listened to all her ideas about life. He could use all that against her, and she would eventually give in, smile and leave all the thinking to him.

She could never escape.

· · ·

Barry felt like the end of the chase was near. It was plain that Billie was on foot, walking from place to place in Hilo. She had some place to sleep nearby. Based on the one traffic camera photo of her and the shops she'd visited, he needed to set up surveillance of the string of cabins people could rent along the highway leading south out of town. He could park at the Makalika Gap, where a lava flow three hundred years previously had nearly destroyed Hilo. The highway had been rebuilt at the gap, and if Billie had found a cheap cabin to the south, she would have to walk through the narrow strip or else bushwhack through the woods that had grown up in that area if she wanted to return to the main parts of Hilo to keep looking for a job.

Of course he hoped she would give up and contact him. He glanced at the computer but there was no sign that she'd replied to his last message. Probably, he would have to track her down, hopefully at her cabin, out of the public eye. He didn't relish the confrontation, although he had no fear that she would be able to evade him again.

As sunset approached, he purchased snacks and camped in his vehicle at the best parking space he could find near the gap. He surveyed the road with his binoculars and tried to guess which cabin was hers. From time to time, he did a little research, locating the booking services that rented the cabins. They were all closed until morning.

With his binoculars, he could check passing traffic. There was always the possibility that she had acquired allies, like that tourist family in San Diego. Nobody looked like Billie.

By sunrise, he was feeling the effects of a nighttime stakeout, but it didn't affect his alertness. A few hours later, he was getting worried. There was no sign of her at all, and it wasn't like Billie to sleep in. Had his message to her made her give up her search for a job? Was she trying to sneak out some other way, perhaps along the beach or even going farther south?

He made contact with the cabin rental service and soon enough deduced which cabin was hers. He drove there quickly.

The door wasn't locked.

"Billie? Are you in?" He tried to sound cheerful.

The place was quiet. It barely showed signs of her presence. Her travel bag—the one he'd seen her use on the airport videos—was still sitting upright by her bed. Her computer was open and the display was lit up.

He hurriedly took a look, hoping that she had senselessly left it unlocked.

On the display was a control box. It said, "Send Message to 'Daddy' in 34 minutes." He quickly stabbed the button that said, "Send Now." The display flashed "Sent" and then went dark.

He tapped the keyboard, but it had auto locked.

There was a tightness in his chest. Something was very wrong. Billie would never have left her computer behind, especially if she knew he was hot on her trail. Maybe she'd abandon her luggage, but not the computer. He grabbed it and ran out to his vehicle.

On his computer was the message alert. He stabbed at it.

"Daddy, you'll never catch me. I'll never come back and be your stupid little daughter. Nor will I ever be your second attempt at Beta. You're a monster and a mass murderer and now that I know your secret, I can't ever even look at you again.

"You've proved that you could track me down. I tried, but I failed to have a life of my own, but I won't ever be YOURS! I know only one place to escape. One place you can never follow. And I'll make sure that there's not even dust for you to use to make another Beta!"

He puzzled over the short text. It sounded almost....

He shook his head. She wouldn't kill herself! How could she?

The words "mass murderer" glared at him. Had she somehow deduced that he was the originator of the Plague of history? How could she figure that out? He'd never told anyone. He'd never written it down anywhere.

He had a flicker of memory. There had been that one girl who had invaded his place in Denver and drugged him. He'd let something slip with her, but then she'd immediately managed to kill herself in a vain attempt to stop the disease's progress.

No, nobody knew it was him.

But something had set her off, and he just hoped he was misinterpreting her text.

He read it again, focusing on "one place to escape" and "not even dust" trying to put it all together.

He looked out the window. He grabbed his binoculars and saw a distant figure making her way through the woods, approaching a small fenced off area. It was Billie!

The map gave him worrisome details. That was a small airport. Hover-capable craft flew out of there to give tourists a close-up view of the active lava flows.

"No! Billie, you can't!"

He raced down the highway, having to loop the long way around to get to the airport. He barely stayed on the road, the tires squealing as he made too-sharp turns. There was a gate, but it was open and he raced in.

A pilot, checking his craft prior to a morning flight looked up to see the crazy person jump out and race toward him.

"What's going on?"

Barry pointed across the field. "I just saw someone jump the fence. Look, they're getting in one of your hovers!"

The pilot was shocked that the distant engines rumbled to life and the six rotors started spinning. "Hey!" he yelled, but it was fruitless.

The hover lifted unsteadily, almost skidding sideways into another of the craft.

The pilot glared at Barry. "Who are you?"

"Nobody! But you've got to stop her!"

"How?"

The hover gained some altitude and the obviously inexperienced hijacker took a wobbling course inland.

Barry grabbed the pilot by the arm and locked eyes with him. "We have to chase her! I'll pay ten times your rate, but we've got to go now!"

The pilot hesitated, but the man's clothes and vehicle said money, so he nodded.

They raced to his hover and with just a gesture at the seatbelt, they were soon taking off.

The pilot was on the radio. "Yes, I saw! Somebody jumped the fence. I'm on it."

He looked at Barry. "Who is it?"

"I don't know."

The pilot knew something was wrong. The man's face said he knew something. He knew who it was.

"You have to know something!"

Barry glared, "Just fly! Twenty times and no questions!"

The pilot focused on the chase. "She's headed straight for the volcano."

Barry could see the smoke for himself. He nodded.

His pilot was much more experienced, but Billie was learning quickly. They weren't catching up on her very quickly.

They gained altitude, but Billie was staying close to the ground.

"She's going to have to get higher. The lava causes dangerous updrafts. How good a pilot is she?"

"I don't know."

Climbing up the slopes, heading straight toward the smoking lava cone, Billie's hover was wobbling, trying to stay clear of the ground and any of the minor plumes.

Barry asked, "Can you get closer? Try to force her down?"

The pilot just shook his head. "Kill us both doing that."

"Do something!"

The pilot tried to get a little closer. He had a loudspeaker. He called out. "Watch out for the updrafts! Come on back!"

Billie's hover crested the edge of the pit, over the bright red flowing lava.

Then, almost in slow motion, the hover tilted and turned nearly on edge.

The pilot and Barry cried out, "No!" almost as one.

And then the craft slid straight into the lava pool. The exploding fuel tank was hardly noticeable. Barry screamed.

The End of Barry

Barry was almost catatonic on the trip back. There were questions, both by the pilot and by the police who finally arrived at the little airport.

"I don't know." He said that a hundred times. He didn't really listen to the questions.

He managed to pay his promised bonus without a word, and when the police couldn't get anything from him, he drove away.

Somehow, he stayed on the road, but he didn't know where he was going, taking turns at random. When the warning chime alerted him that his alcohol tank was almost empty, he pulled off the side of the road and stared at the surf splashing up on a black sand beach.

I am alone. It was the most coherent thought in hours. He was alone again. Beta had died again. Billie was gone, hating him to her last breath.

He stepped out onto the black rubble, ripped off his shirt and walked toward the water. He kicked off his shoes and swam as hard as he could out into the Pacific Ocean.

A wave caught him in the face and he choked, the swirling waters pulling him under the surface. He didn't even try to fight it.

The Old Man persona took control. Barry the salesman was just too weak for this. The Warrior woke up, a bare bones persona that was only concerned with survival. He swam back to the surface and fought the waves until he choked up the swallowed seawater, resting on the black sand.

And then the Old Man put the Barry persona away for good. He'd lost centuries after the loss of the original Beta, and he couldn't tolerate that again. Some other less sensitive persona was needed.

Frank Orman blinked and he started hunting for his shoes.

Frank had all the memories, but Billie was just someone from his history and her death was just like all the others that he had observed in his endless life. It was sad, certainly, but he had other priorities right now, like how to get more fuel and get back to the Vermillion. He frowned at his ruined shirt but buttons or not, it was all he had.

Checking the map, he found the nearest town and drove until the tank went dry. A little hike later, he had a enough alcohol to get back on the road.

Onboard the Vermillion, he logged a flight to Panama, but as soon as he was in the air, he changed course to Isla Teresa and the secret base where another frozen embryo of Beta could be put into play.

He didn't rush, taking his time to consider what he should do next.

Raising Billie as his daughter had been a failed strategy. Reviewing all of her messages, it was plain that the change from his daughter to a potential romantic partner was just too big a jump for her. Maybe he should have predicted it.

There were two big problems. The sexual status change was one, but the other was that he was just a bad father. In all his years, he'd avoided most women who already had children. There had been a few cases, but it wasn't a role he was comfortable with. Thinking back over the thirty years with Billie made it clear that he was just killing time through it all until she matured. He wasn't good at it.

The original Beta had raised herself, just like he had done. They had hopped from one foster family to another until they had the skills to go it alone. They were alike.

Much more than the common genetic history, that life development would have made them ideal partners. He knew that several of his identities were attractive romantic partners for the women he'd met. The common history and his pleasing personality should have brought the original Beta to his side. Billie, his daughter, was cursed from the beginning. If he tried the same course over the next thirty years, would a second Billie die rather than join him, too?

The second clone needed a different life history. He shouldn't even try to raise her himself.

. . .

Three years later, Frank rushed to make his last computer entries. The starship Athens was beautiful to human eyes, a round shape designed to maximize the volume that could be transported via the leap drive purchased from the Click, yet flattened to be able to ride on the ocean surface. The upper third was capped in transparent tanstran so that the behemoth riding on the Mediterranean Sea—not too far from its namesake city—looked like a miniature domed city itself.

Frank was already aboard, a crewman specialized in loading and securing cargo, a job he'd done many times in his long life. Interstellar tourism was just an idea for the very rich at this stage of human culture. If he wanted to see the universe, he'd have to pay his way with labor.

But he had plans.

The biggest problem was that the only way to communicate from star to star was by carrying the message on starships. There was no faster-than-light radio. He would be gone for months or years and he had no way to communicate with his organizations on Earth.

One group was taking care of his money. They would be investing and sending regular updates to him. However, he had an Earth-side computer proxy masquerading as him, just to give the illusion that he was constantly watching over his workers.

Another group was taking care of young Elizabeth. The Beth group had been paying for her care since the host mother had been hired to carry her to term. Frank was taking a hands-off approach since the beginning, but the baby still needed someone to pay her way and keep her out of random hazards and callous foster parents alike. There was a general plan to rotate her from one home to another, at least until she took matters into her own hands.

There was another group that were nothing more than historians who packaged up current events and sent the summary to him, where ever he might be.

And he was also composing a message for the Distant Skies travel magazine, the one he'd enjoyed the most.

"I'm leaving today on the Athens and having enjoyed your articles on other worlds, I'd like to send you my own photos and tales of my travels. Expect to receive them under the Wandering Kid byline."

Maybe he could turn this into a regular thing, but he had to send off this first episode today before the Athens made its first leap. He was in a frantic rush to stay on top of his official job as well and get all the messages sent before it was too late.

The warning sirens started, giving spectators plenty of time to get clear. Underwater alerts were giving any local merfolk the same warning. Take off, with such a massive craft sending ocean spray in all directions, would swamp any smaller craft in the neighborhood. Trial flights during construction had confirmed that the cirrance pulses were so loud that people could be severely injured if they were too close.

No other galactic race had starships that even attempted a planetary landing, but then no other race had the human-invented high-power TP beams that could make it possible.

It was expected that most of the time, this starship would be loaded and unloaded via smaller boats in space, just like all the other starships. But the Athens had grander plans, including transferring bulk cargo directly from one world to another without using an endless stream of boats.

There was even negotiations with the Kwish home world to see if a landing there on their ocean would be possible. The aquatic species had its reservations, due to the cirrance issue.

In any case, ocean worlds were common enough that the Athens had high hopes for its future profitability.

Then liftoff happened, and Frank was at his duty station, making sure that none of the cargo shifted. He had done his job. Everything was stable.

However, on the upper decks, he had several strategically-placed cameras, taking breathtaking videos of the flight out of the atmosphere and the slow rotation to show the Earth below and the space cities in the distance. Multitasking, he did his final edits for his first travel episode and sent it off while never taking an eye off of his cargo status displays.

And then, the Athens leapt across the impossible distance to the second planet of Delta Pavonis where half the passengers and a third of the cargo were destined to join a new colony where French-speaking lingual separatists were hoping to create a pure New France. His cameras caught that approach as well.

Frank had brushed up on the dying language so that he was sure to be able to visit and take his travel pictures on the new human world. He was a tourist now, and he was taking no half-measures. He'd be touring the universe until Elizabeth was an adult and he could meet her for the first time. He'd have plenty of tales to share with her.

Dell's Visit

Ohen bar Clay struggled awake, conscious of his granddaughter humming to herself in the kitchen. Hermione was enjoying the solitude as the Lunar dawnwind passed its peak and even the early light hadn't yet brought the others out to face the day.

Her thoughts were interesting, never even imagining such a thing as a telepath reading her secrets. It was certainly incomprehensible that her feeble grandfather was one.

But she wasn't thinking of him at all.

What shall I name her? She hadn't even told Welly yet. She wanted the perfect moment to spring the news.

Mom said she was named Helen because Gran was an academic and named her after the most beautiful woman in the world, and then I was named after Helen of Troy's daughter, so I could think of myself as a princess.

Ohen mused on the changes that had happened in his lifetime. Although Luna was still officially an empire, the rapid industrialization and interworld commerce had changed everything. Mars might still be a real empire with competing royal families, but Alice's family had traded their royal status for more stability, ceding the real ruling authority to the Council. His own family was so far out of any royal family tree that no one thought they were anything but a merchant family.

As he struggled to get out of bed, he grumbled, but not loud enough to be heard. *If this wasn't Lunar gravity, I'd be trapped in this bed forever. I'm in really bad shape.*

He was tempted to invite a Healer from New Ha to come for a "social visit" and see if she could do something about his deterioration, but he didn't have any real excuse for that. People got old and his clan, the descendants of Omelia, tended to age sooner than most U'tanse due to their size. *Live as a giant, and die younger;* although he could hardly be called young by anyone.

By the time he got dressed, Hermione had come up with a couple of girl names and a couple of boy names as well, although she hoped for a daughter.

Ohen's clairvoyance had already determined that she would get her wish, but he couldn't share that information. The Pledge of the U'tanse was even his idea, and he couldn't break it. Any U'tanse who came to live among baseline humanity had to pledge to never reveal their psychic gifts, to make sure that all their children were tenners, and give up their copy of the Book.

That last one had been harder than he'd realized. U'tanse carried a copy of the Book as part of their identity. Giving it up so that it might never fall into the hands of ordinary humans who would then discover the psychic gifts of the U'tanse was important, but it was a big psychological step as well. If you're going to live with humans and have human children, then you're not really U'tanse anymore.

So Ohen smiled, and as he took halting steps into the kitchen to greet his granddaughter, he resolved to keep all of her secrets to himself.

"There you are, Sleepyhead. Pancakes in two minutes."

"Raspberry jelly?" He sat down at the table.

"Of course. You remind me every day."

Ohen was so grateful Hermione had come to help. He'd been a little lost when Alice died and he was reluctant to ask his children to pause their lives to come help him. Helen and her husband John were running a shipping company in Cleomedes. Hermione and her new husband, Welly, had been struggling to make ends meet in the city and were intrigued with the offer to keep his house going in Stampz. Welly was finding his way doing some light gardening on the property and working at the cotton gin. Ohen used just enough of his telepathic snooping to make sure the young couple weren't actually suffering in silence just for his sake.

Hermione said, "Dell is coming for a visit in a few hours."

He grunted. "Thanks for the reminder."

The winds were dying down when the time came. Ohen noticed the approaching craft via his clairvoyance well before his fading eyesight picked it up, approaching from the Gate.

"Can you hear it?" asked Hermione as she searched the skies to the east.

"Not yet, but it's supposed to be noisy."

But, soon enough the hover showed up in the sky overhead and settled down on the circular patch of grass that no longer had any visits from his boat, sold off when Ohen could no longer fly it himself.

Ohen leaned on his cane and peered at the craft. It was obviously imported from Earth—using one of those alcohol-fueled engines. He wished he had the time and energy to poke around inside, but he was just fooling himself. His engineering days were long passed.

Dell looked so much like his father Samuel that it was startling when he stepped out. They shook hands and Hermione gave her cousin a hug. They sat at an outdoor table under a trellis covered in grape vines.

Ohen looked his grandson over. "So, the first Lunar astronomer is heading for the stars."

Dell gave a slight smile. "I get that all the time—an astronomer on a cloud-covered world where we can barely get a clear view of the sun or the Earth."

Ohen shook his head. "Not surprising to me. Sammy was fascinated with the stars when we took him into space."

Dell laughed. "I got hooked after a few trips with Dad. He's off-world more often than not, these days. When I couldn't talk him into taking me along on his business trip one time, Grandma Alice showed me a book on radio telescopes and it's been downhill from then on."

"I've heard you're working on some kind of interstellar radio telescope?"

Dell leaned closer, the excitement spilling off of him. "Yes! It's going to be unprecedented. Radio, visual light, X-rays and maybe even if we're lucky, detecting TP emissions. We're going to have identical facilities at several places in the Solar system, a couple in the Ko system and one on the Uuaa system. We'll be recording everything and then transporting the data via starship to a central computer system near Ceres."

Ohen nodded. "Synthetic aperture."

"You get it! It'll be like looking at the galaxy with a lens a hundred light years across, once we get it all synchronized. We should be able to detect objects down to asteroid size no matter where they are, even if they are in deep space far from a star."

Dell shook his head. "I'm so lucky I have U'tanse heritage. It's practically impossible to get a travel visa to the Ko system without it. The consortium is always in communication with the U'tanse, but we hardly ever get to meet with them face to face. Somebody had to go to help with the coordination and setup in the Ko and Uuaa systems, and I'm just glad it's me."

Hermione shook her head. "If you're going to talk tech stuff, I need to go deal with the laundry. Dell, do you need anything done?"

"I'm just starting out. No dirty laundry yet."

"Don't keep the old guy up for too long. He takes a lot of naps."

When she walked off, Ohen smiled. "It's been great to have her here. But don't worry about my naps. I'm happy to get this chance to talk to you. Do you need any pointers?"

Dell chuckled. "Of course. I feel out of my depth here. I don't know anything about the U'tanse, really. Everyone comes to me with questions but just have to tell them that I've only met you a few times at family gatherings and you weren't one to tell people about your adventures."

Ohen shrugged. "Here's your chance. What do you know about the U'tanse?"

"I don't know much. They were captured by the Cerik back at the time of the Betelgeuse supernova and somehow rediscovered the Solar system centuries later. Since then, U'tanse have been reclusive. We trade and a few isolated individuals like my grandfather have settled here, but the rest is just speculation."

"Oh, tell me. I love a good theory. The wilder the better."

The edge of Dell's mouth twisted a bit. "Okay. Hmm. The most common theory is that the U'tanse panicked over the Plague and are deathly afraid of diseases.

"Another one is that the U'tanse aren't really human, just parallel evolution that produced human lookalikes and that the Cerik story isn't real."

Ohen was smiling and nodding. "And you say?"

Dell sighed. "It depends. Some people know I'm one-quarter U'tanse, but most don't, or didn't until I signed up for this trip. I never tried to convince people we're not really aliens."

"Any other theories?"

"Not many. U'tanse are really psychics is one. They are planning an invasion, but taking a really long time doing their research. Other things like that. There are pictures of you, you know, from when you were younger. Having a U'tanse that's a head taller than anyone else has fueled a few conspiracy theories."

As they talked, Ohen got the impression that there wasn't really much gossip about the U'tanse because they had the real Galactic aliens hogging all the most exotic speculation.

Ohen started telling Dell about what to expect when he went to New Ha for his physical examination and evaluation before the starship showed up to take him to the Ko system.

"At some point, they're going to ask you to agree to a secrecy pledge and you should be prepared for that. There are U'tanse secrets and you need to be comfortable with that."

Dell shrugged. "I'm Alpine. Secrets are what I've grown up with. I'm sure I can keep some more."

Ohen nodded. "Tell me about it. Don't hold it against me when you learn all the deep dark U'tanse secrets I've been keeping from you.

"On that Alpine issue, do you have a girlfriend?"

"Sadly, I've just been that quirky academic tending my radio telescopes with nothing much to show for it. I have a couple of female friends, but having a big secret like the Alpine gene is a big damper on trying to get more social."

"I know a few families here in Stampz that are already in the know."

"Yeah, but now isn't the time. I'll be leaving for New Ha in a few days."

Ohen told him more about Ha, at least what he remembered from when he was young.

"I wouldn't plan on getting to visit the planet Ko. Nearly all of the U'tanse civilization is on the moon of Ha or other space settlements. Down on Ko, there's always the chance you'd encounter a Cerik and you don't want to get eaten. They really are monsters—a lot more beast-like than the Galactics we've encountered."

Dell frowned. "That's one thing I've never understood. How did beast-like monsters come here and invade Earth?"

Ohen talked about the Delense and how they engineered the machines for their masters. "Even the Cerik could understand that if they slashed their claws a certain way, that they could make their machines fly. It doesn't mean that they ever had the capability to understand anything about those machines."

"So," Dell puzzled it out, "the Delense were Galactic-like engineers, but yet they were slaves to the beasts?"

"Never doubt the power of a warrior with bloodlust. And that reminds me of something else you need to know about the U'tanse. We're all pacifists. We can't fight. More than fearing diseases like the Plague, the U'tanse fear mainline humanity's ability to fight wars and slaughter their enemies."

"Yes, but at the core, we're all human. We can all be pacifists or warriors, can't we?"

"Don't ignore training. All U'tanse learned that trait. When I was dropped into warlike Mars and I attempted to fight, it about killed me. Even playing the strategist and keeping the real battle far away from me wasn't enough. I moved to Luna and never went back."

Dell sighed. "I guess visiting the U'tanse will be a little different from coming here to Stampz and listening to my grandfather."

Ohen shrugged. "Who knows? I've lived most of my life here, but I was raised on Ha. I envy your trip. I originally intended to go off on a short excursion and then come home again. I never went back."

Dell considered it. "I guess it could happen to me, too."

"Well, other than that pesky Alpine gene thing."

They nodded.

Hermione came back and gave Ohen the excuse to take his nap. The cousins chatted a while. Dell was wondering when he'd ever get back to see them again.

Ohen knew the chances were slight that he'd see Dell again. His clairvoyance gave him bad news every time he examined his health closely. If he had to guess, he'd have another stroke within the year, and there was no guarantee he'd be able to dissolve it quickly enough like last time.

He was so grateful Dell made the stop to see him before he left.

Spaceport Lumen

He was working under the name Sam Kidd—he favored that surname more than was wise—although that persona was sleeping. Kidd was the tourist and wrote the travel guides, but his active persona, Luther, was closer to his baseline. He needed the experience of a more mature personality while he was at the spaceport. Kidd would just visit the shops and restaurants and maybe write a few hundred words about them. Luther needed to take advantage of the Earth ships visiting Spaceport Lumen.

Lumen was just the human label for the place. Starships from a dozen cultures visited the orbital station about a light-second from the ice-covered planet below. There were more than a dozen habitats linked together with walkable tunnels, making the whole of the spaceport look like a fat snowflake.

The Sissen Galactics who lived on the planet down below had an extensive network of cities under the ice, built to last another ten thousand years or so until the ice began to melt. The Sissen hadn't been self-sufficient for a long time, depending on Galactic trade to bring them food, trading coordinates in exchange.

Sissen ships had been scouting all through the galaxy, discovering habitable planets, valuable asteroidal belts, and anything else that other races might want to exploit. The Sissen had no inclination to make colonies of their own and traded their information for goods to keep their home planet thriving.

From what Luther could tell, there were three human starships that made regular stops at Lumen. He needed to get his personal computer close enough to one of those ships, or at least their shuttle boats. Once in radio range, all the messages that were addressed to him could be downloaded.

In addition, he'd send Kidd's latest travel articles back to Distant Skies on Earth. None of the transmissions were instant.

A series of messages arrived, some over three years old, having been relayed from one ship to another all this time. He was honestly surprised that the system could predict where he might be in order to get his messages sent in the right direction, but then again, the forwarding system had been in place for centuries, being improved all that time, so he just decided to treat it as magic and didn't worry about the details.

It was frustrating that there was nothing really current. The most recent financial reports were two years old and the latest news about Elizabeth was that she was last seen living on her own in Paris, pretending to be twelve and working as a courier. His spies were ready to assist her if necessary, but she hadn't needed help in the last five years. The spies were fired and new ones hired on a periodic basis to keep them from realizing her true age and that seemed to be working okay. He just wished the reports could find him more quickly.

Once all the messages were transferred and he had a few minutes to read them, Luther relaxed and the Sam Kidd persona woke up, realizing he'd just had another of his blackouts.

He was surprised to see that his articles had been sent. Distant Skies was always happy to get his work and they paid well, even if it seemed to take forever for the money to show up in his computer account.

Sometimes he had the urge to change ships and head back to Earth, but really, he was just a tourist at heart and there was nothing on Earth that interested him. And right now he was in an exotic spaceport, built long ago by other races and he really needed to do some shopping and take some pictures for his next article.

The *lingua franca* of the station was the Sissen tongue so he made sure his translator earpieces were loaded with the proper data set and then wandered through the shops. Pocket money in this part of the galaxy were metal tokens inscribed with a verification code. He kept a bit of it handy, just for occasions like this when a shop appeared. His current ship, the Starship Mombasa, had an exchange station for people like him where he could cash out some of his computer credits for what the locals used. It was one of the reasons he'd last switched to this ship.

A wide, leathery shopkeeper saw him enter and tapped a strap on his apron, probably activating his own translator. His circular mouth quivered and Kidd's earpieces said, "Greetings traveler. Can I interest you in Hurf hand-toys or Jellen ticklers? They're at reduced prices this week since I just stocked up."

Kidd held up his empty palm. "Perhaps. I would love to see what's on your shelves."

The shopkeeper waved with his double-articulated arm, not moving from his position. Kidd wasn't sure whether he was mobility restricted or whether he was just considerate of the private space of his customers. He wasn't even sure if the species had legs.

After purchasing a Hurf flicker, just to keep the shopkeeper happy with him, he browsed deeper into the shop, chatting and trying to get more information about where things came from.

"Are these jewels?" He pointed at three gray stones, carefully presented behind transparent windows in what looked like a pressure chamber.

"Ah, you have an eye for the exceptional. Those are worth more than my shop. Their documentation claims they came from the Pit. Nobody knows what they are, but strange energy has been detected from them under the right conditions."

"Why are they here in your shop?"

The shopkeeper stroked his sloping forehead. It gave off a rasping sound. "It was a trade, a ship arrived from inward with nothing much to sell and not enough resources to get back home. Several of us got together and took what they had. The Sissen bought their travel logs. They restocked and left. That's about all I know about it."

"Then tell me about the Pit. I've heard it mentioned before, but no details."

Nobody knew much about it. There was a place, somewhere inward, called the Pit or the Hole. Riches beyond imagining were there for the taking, but nobody had found it, although there were always rumors.

Anything odd, like these gray stones, were ascribed to the Pit, but it was all legend and hearsay.

"Inward, you say?" Closer to the center of the galaxy, the stars were closer together.

The shopkeeper waved his arm. "That's what they always say, but where exactly, no one knows. The galaxy is a big place."

Probably the Pit was just as mythological as Eldorado and Shangri-La on Earth, but the reality of those stones made it intriguing. It seemed that at least three different alien species talked about the Pit, which made the origin of the legend even more puzzling.

He asked their price and shivered. "Not within my budget."

The shopkeeper rubbed his forehead. "That's what they all say."

Kidd purchased another trinket to share with his co-workers, but his mind was made up. Earth could wait a few more years. He'd need to find some other human-crewed starship that was heading inward, closer to wherever the Pit was.

He had no objection to working on an alien vessel, but there was always the issue of the right food and environment. And hardly any of the other races had human-style computers that could be used to relay his messages. For now, it was just safer to stay with the humans.

Kidd had big grin on his face as he made his way back to the Starship Mombasa. He was off to hunt for Shangri-La again.

Balecat

It was the girl. Sam Kidd shook his head as they lashed his left arm to the tall wicker structure. He had plenty of experience. He shouldn't get himself into situations like this. Anne Lex, a school teacher in her early twenties, was being secured as he was, one arm to the front of the tall contraption. In the flickering torch light, her wide eyes were turning right and left looking for some friendly face in this ominous crowd. The adults were flat faced—showing no emotion at all, unless it was in the fact that two thirds of them never looked in his direction.

The fifteen year olds, the real focus of this ceremony, were not tied, just standing uneasy in their place. There were a dozen of their number, and every one of them were remembering the two who vanished, a year ago this day.

Sam locked eyes with Ian, one of the Clan Mooren children who had been in Anne's one-room school when he had come to visit earlier today. Ian looked back with the same sad, flat expression that had so puzzled him then. If the boy knew what he was facing this evening, then that sadness wasn't such a mystery any more.

Sam's bound arm moved with the wooden crossbeam, as several of the villagers climbed up on the thing. It creaked, and shifted. *The whole thing moves.*

Suddenly he understood what was due to happen. The wood and wicker structure, three times his height and shaped like some kind of giant cat, was on wheels. He and Anne, and the teenagers, were on a long ramp below it, a road with high walls on both sides for as far as he could see. Once this thing started moving, it would be a race for the children to stay ahead of it.

Tied as they were, the two adults would be dragged to their deaths.

A man carrying a torch came close, on the top of the wall overhead. It was the Ringerman, the head of the community. He chimed the bell and then addressed the children.

"We have come this world, and this valley, to praise God with our sweat and to purify our seed from the guilt of Irowik."

The children and the whole village chanted back, "We are unworthy of the sun."

The Ringerman continued, "We work under the sun, but the night would not have us either. From the first season in this valley, our children have been lost to the balecat."

He spread his arms, "All here assembled have faced the balecat. We have all run from his wrath and heard his roar, calling for our blood.

"Tonight, it is your turn. Tonight, you must run hard and escape his jaws, so that the Clan Mooren may be made stronger by your number." He turned as if to go.

Sam called out, "Hey! I came to this world to write a travel book. Anne Lex came from the Port to teach your children how to read. Why are we here?"

The Ringerman, looked distastefully down on the two of them, "I warned you! I told you to be gone from this valley by nightfall.

"I told you," pointing at the schoolteacher, "to stay put in your house at night, every night! We didn't invite you here. You Coopers think the whole world revolves around Port. Our children are taught what they need to know, not the needs of Port. Now your blood is on your own heads!"

He waved up a the people in the big wicker cat. A trio of voices started making growls like a large cat. Kidd felt it start to move. He moved his feet, but tied like he was, he couldn't even walk in a straight line. Anne screamed in terror as she suddenly realized what was happening. She gave him a pleading look, but he was in the same position she was. The road down to the river was rough and rocky, and they would be torn to bloody meat long before it rolled to a stop.

Sam Kidd started to run in earnest as the cat started gaining speed on the incline. The world went gray as he blacked out.

...

The Warrior persona forced his way into full consciousness. With his arm tied, the situation was critical, but he spent two precious seconds looking around in all directions. The villagers were running along the top of the left wall, carrying their torches. Escape that way would mean recapture. The teenagers were moving well, accelerating faster than the wheeled cart with its top-heavy payload. It would be several seconds before the cart would start to gain on them. The road ahead narrowed slightly just where the large round threshing house was built.

Timing would be tight. He started a count down.

Five. He concentrated on getting his feet moving high and fast. The girl was struggling. In her long skirt, it was even harder for her to keep her feet under her. He could do nothing to help her yet.

Four. With his free hand, he ran his free index finger down the front of his shirt, and fingered the button one up from the bottom.

Three. He snapped the button loose. Among the thread fibers that had secured it was a whisker of wire thinner than a hair. Snapping that wire killed a flea-power magnetic field that surrounded a few "atoms" of one of the more unstable "elements" from the Pit.

Two. He reached far over, and wedged the button into a gap in the wicker with enough strength that his finger would be bruised for days.

One. He pulled his body as far away from the button as his strength could manage.

The button was made as an assassin's tool. The "atoms" from the Pit collapsed in a silent explosion, sending a pulse of scrambled physics half a meter in all directions. All normal matter within that sphere lost its ability to form chemical bonds for a fraction of a second. For that brief instant, everything was cold plasma, every atom heading in a random direction. Normal physical laws returned in a flash, and matter recombined. But now, everything was slightly scrambled, and the crystals in the iron and the cell walls of the wood no longer held any of their former strength.

Zero. A chunk of the wagon, including the wooden beam he was tied to and part of the corner wagon wheel, turned into dust. Warrior pulled hard on the beam and broke it free. He pulled a decorative blue inlay from his beltbuckle and using its razor-sharp edge, cut free the bindings on his arm.

The cart lurched and shuddered as the broken wheel fragmented. It hit the wall hard and started to tilt over. As the voices above stopped their growls and became shrieks, the Warrior freed the girl, and then slipped the inlay back into his belt buckle. Before she had time to react, he lifted her and began running.

The wicker cat behind them crunched against the wall and the whole structure started to tilt over. There were shouts from the side, as villagers found themselves beneath the toppling balecat.

The Warrior found the right spot on the wall opposite the commotion and lifted himself and the girl out of the roadway. Not stopping to look back, he began a high-speed run, carrying his struggling burden across his shoulders.

It was dark, but the field was harvested, and he could match his stride to the tops of the furrows. The Warrior kept conscious until they reached the trees at the edge of the field.

...

Sam Kidd put his hand to his temple—another of his blackouts, but somehow they escaped. "Are you okay?" he asked her.

Anne was struggling to breathe. He was concerned that she was injured. He put his hand on her shoulder feeling the shaking of her body.

She gasped a loud intake of air and then forced out the words, "How dare they do that to my children!"

Sam shook his head, "They were doing it to *their* children."

She glared at him. Even in the dim light of the star trails overhead, he winced at her ferocity.

"I don't know how it is out there, Mr. 'I've-been-to-over-a-dozen-star-systems', but on Julie-Baby, we value our children."

He put his hand on her elbow and started her moving up the tree-covered ravine. He didn't want to be where the villagers might find them.

"Are you sure," he asked, "that this isn't something the other farming settlements might come up with? Weren't they all settled by the same Tupelo sect?"

She shook her head, "No. All of the other towns participate in the festival circuit. They intermarry—I ought to know, the only boy worth anything in Port married a Charleston girl last summer." She layered some bitterness into the words. "I thought this teacher program would let me get out and meet more people. But they've kept me bottled up in the school house this whole time, and the first time I break one of their silly rules, they try to kill me. I was just starting to understand them!"

He nodded. Her history explained why she latched on to him the instant he walked into this valley yesterday. After months of isolation in his tiny cabin on the transport ship, she had been a joy to talk to, and he had been happy to come to her class and talk to her students. He thought she liked him.

But now he looked at her carefully. Was she strong enough to make a hike? The land was fairly tame, with no large animals or poisonous beasts. If they could make it over this pass and hike the back way over to the metal production plant, they could get back to Port in a week or so, plenty of time to catch the same grain transport out that he arrived on, rather than wait the three months for the next one.

It would put a crimp in his planet-to-planet hopscotch path toward the Pit, but he had the time. It would be good to have a companion again. His past was a blur, but he knew that it had been alone for a long time.

The real question was; should he push for it? Could he charm her enough? Would she go with him?

...

She noticed him feeling his side. "Are you hurt?"

He paused and looked back down the way they had come. The flickering lights had vanished an hour before. Somehow he doubted that they were following.

"No, I just have some muscle aches. I get them every so often. I will be all right."

She nodded, "I am not surprised, the way you ran. You are a lot stronger than you look."

Kidd let the cryptic comment pass. It did no good to ask other people what happened when he blacked out. He turned his thoughts toward their predicament.

He asked, "Do you know whether there is a path we can follow when it gets light. This looks like a game trail more than anything. I would hate to get lost and come back into the same valley."

"No, I don't think anyone goes anywhere except to trade their grain to Port storage. Those people really are frightened of the dark. I have seen it in the children. The older ones are worse than the little ones."

"So we have to avoid the road. I have a good direction sense, but if we could avoid a mountain or two, it would save us days."

She sighed. "I can't wait to get back to the real world. When I tell Port what has been going on out here, things will change! Believe me."

He didn't, but he didn't say that. "The Ringerman knows that. That is why you had to be killed."

She was silent for a moment, before a sob broke the silence.

"I was just worried about Ian! His sister was crying. That was why I was out after dark. Is that enough to kill me for?"

He put his arm around her shoulder and pulled her close. She clung to him. He felt her warmth as she sobbed out her anger and fear.

...

"What is that?" he asked.

Anne started awake. She was suddenly embarrassed to be in his arms and stood up, shaking her skirt free of imaginary dirt. From the stars, it had to be nearly midnight.

"There it is again."

"What?" she asked.

"That sound." He stood up, attentive to the night.

After a moment, they both heard it, a growl, something like the villagers made during the ceremony.

She grabbed his arm. "They are coming after us."

He pushed her, getting them moving. The trail they had been following was still barely visible to their dark-adapted eyes.

"What do you know," he asked, "about this 'guilt of Irowik'?"

"Not much. Almost all of the farming settlements have it in their history, but no one talks about it. We Coopers were hired to do the Port administration and marketing. We have always been outsiders on Julie-Baby."

Sam thought a moment before continuing. He didn't want to terrify her.

"I had thought that this balecat ceremony was part of the Irowik sect, but you seem sure that this isn't some sort of rite-of-passage thing in the other settlements."

"Of course not. I have friends in Rellis-town. Good friends. They would never tolerate anything like that."

He reserved his comment on that. He had seen many cultures and many different ghastly practices—often done by really nice people.

"Okay, suppose that this settlement has come up against something different. Maybe there is a real balecat. It would explain their fear of the dark."

He could see her stiffen up as she considered the idea.

"Julie-Baby doesn't have any large animals," she asserted. Everybody knew that.

"Why is that?"

"You think...." she asked.

"Earth has no large animals anymore either."

"A real balecat?"

"Yes. This game trail we are following. Look how wide it is. I think that we might have a large cat coming up behind us. I think we need to find some place to defend ourselves."

Linguist

The dark made every overhang look like a bottomless pit, and they did a great deal of patting the darkness, feeling the rock. If the trail hadn't lead directly into the cave, they might have missed it entirely.

He sniffed, some animal scent, "This is its den."

"Then we have to get out."

"That would do no good. A predator will already have our scent. We have rock to our backs. We can defend this place."

At his suggestion, they collected some branches and he asked for a strip of cloth from her skirt. There was a little piece of metal he didn't remember having in his pocket, and it sparked nicely. The light of the fire lit up the mouth of the cave. It might just be enough to hold off any balecat until morning light.

At least that is what he told her, letting her rest her head against his shoulder.

It would do no good to point out the reflective eyes watching them on the other side of the flickering blaze.

...

The Warrior felt the girl beginning to wake up. He picked up another stone from the pile and tossed it hard and straight before switching back to the other persona.

...

Sam Kidd felt the follow-through of his throw, and was pleased to see the balecat dance to the side to avoid the missile.

"What are you doing?"

"Throwing rocks at the balecat."

She tensed, and leaned forward, "Where?"

"Between the two trees to the left."

She took in a breath, and then reached for a branch at her feet.

"Don't add to the fire yet."

"Why?"

"We need to stretch the fuel. We have to gamble that it will go find other shelter when the sun comes up. Until then, the fire seems to keep it at bay."

She nodded, but held on to the branch.

"I suppose this will make an interesting chapter in your book," she commented with a flutter in her voice.

He picked up a rock as the eyes crept closer. That stopped the progress. It was a smart beast.

"No. This is not the kind of thing to put in a travel book."

"Why not?"

"The people who read my books will never travel off their own world, but will read my tales to satisfy the fantasies they tell themselves. I'll tell them the wonderful sights they would see, and the odd but pleasant differences in culture. No one wants my adventures, and especially no one wants to read what's wrong with the alien worlds."

"Why not? I would want to know everything."

"Are you sure? Do you want to travel?"

"Oh yes! I have dreamed of it forever. I lived in Port. Every few months there was this huge magical ship coming down from the sky, and then the roar and the dust as the granaries are pumped up into the ships. It was the most exciting part of life. And when Port administration let a captain come into town, they were always so strange. Their clothes were nothing like what we wore. They talked in such funny ways."

Sam fingered the rock in his hand, but the balecat didn't seem to want to move in.

"Did you know that there are thirty to fifty crewmen on those ships? Did you ever wonder why they never came into town?"

"Well... I knew that there were other people in the ships... No. Tell me. Why didn't they come into town?"

He balanced the rock in his hand, turning over an idea that just seemed to pop into his head.

"Your Port administration doesn't allow it. The crew can go visit a very nice beach where there are visitor's quarters maintained for them, but they are not wanted in Port or any of the settlement towns. I had to make special arrangements to make my solitary hike out into the countryside."

"But why would they do that? We Port people are not so unfriendly."

He nodded, "And nine months after the crewmen met with the friendly Port people, girls like you and your friends would start to have babies with strange-colored skins and hair and eyes that did match up with any of the local boys."

"No," she protested.

"You do know how babies happen?"

She squirmed with embarrassment, "Yes. Of course. I know all that."

"Don't suppose the crewmen are saints. Many of them spend the whole trip dreaming of being with a beautiful girl in the local ports.

"And you must be totally honest—have you had any romantic thoughts about me these two days we have been together?"

"No!" she protested, but she was flushed and nearly incoherent with embarrassment.

"Okay, but you can certainly see that it would happen—a crewman desperate to be close to any pretty face, and a Port girl fascinated by the idea of far away places and the engaging smile of an unattached man?"

She nodded.

"Do you still want to know all the bad things about the other worlds?"

She didn't answer. He nodded.

"Now, one more thing," he continued in the same tone of voice, "I am now going to throw a rock at our balecat."

The cat's eyes flickered and jumped to the side.

"When," she asked, "when are you going to throw the rock?"

Sam stood up and stared across the fire. "You, balecat! I know you can understand what I am saying. Come closer to the light so I can see you better."

"What! Are you saying it can understand us?"

He nodded, "At least some parts of what I am saying. It stopped to listen as I was talking to you, and it jumped when I threatened to throw a rock at it. It has been very cautious and patient, waiting for us to make a mistake. Think about it! The balecat has to be the dominant life form on this planet to have wiped out all larger species, and it must be very smart to have kept its presence so well concealed."

Sam held up his rock, and allowed it to drop to his feet.

They stared out into the dark, and after a minute, the balecat stepped cautiously out of the shadows. It was half again larger than an African lion and black like a panther. Its head was disproportionately large.

"The light," its voice was a faintly voiced hiss, "it is too bright."

...

Sam moved quickly to stack several rocks on the far side of the fire to give the balecat a shadow from the direct light. It flickered away into the trees the instant he put his hand on the rocks, but it was quickly back when it understood what he was doing.

He addressed it again, "We are very surprised to find that you are a person."

The balecat hissed, "Ha!"

"You don't like the word?"

"I am not a person. I am a god."

Sam Kidd relaxed against the rock wall. It was important to be non-threatening. He had to get it to talk.

"Have you taught yourself our language, or did you have help?"

"That is one of my jobs. I listen and watch."

He noted the answer. "You are very good, especially since you have to force your voice to sound like those of our people."

"Thank you. It is pleasant to actually speak your words to their owners."

"So you teach others of your kind?"

"We exchange our understanding."

"In my words, you are a linguist. That is a kind of scientist. One that works to understand language."

The balecat eased down to a resting position. It asked, "A scientist is a learner?"

"Yes, although all people learn, some are allowed to spend their time learning, instead of gathering food or other tasks. A scientist is one of those."

Anne moved closer to him, listening intently. He continued, "However, your use of the terms 'people' and 'god' may be incorrect."

"I use them as the people of the village use them."

"But they are mistaken. A god is not a creature who is pained by the light. A god is not a creature who must dodge rocks. You are an intelligent creature. In my use of the words, that makes you a person."

Anne asked, "Are you going to eat us?"

The balecat moved its massive head slowly from side to side in what looked to be an imitation of a human shake, "No. I do not eat your kind. You are tainted meat. I will use your bodies to attract game to my lures, but I won't eat you."

...

Sam thought fast. He needed more information. He had to keep the balecat talking. Anne now had a tight grip on his arm.

"You can understand that we don't look forward to the idea of being killed."

"I am sorry, but being a linguist is just one of my tasks. Another is to make sure that none of your kind escape to the surrounding valleys."

"I can understand that. However, I feel confident that we can work together to find a solution that you would be comfortable with, and one that would keep us alive.

"For example, we could go back down into the valley, and head back on the human roads?"

"Again, I am sorry, but one of my tasks is to limit the knowledge your kind have of balecats. I can see no help for you."

"But why?" Anne cried. "Why can't you let us go? I don't want to die."

The balecat looked from the male to her, and then back again. "We watched when the first of your kind arrived from the sky. We thought it might be interesting to let you stay. So many of the larger prey animals have been made extinct as our numbers expanded. We thought you might be cultivated.

"But instead of arriving in small numbers, you landed with huge ships and blasted your valleys to ash and poisoned the soil. Many died in the flame and we suddenly realized that in spite of your small size and no teeth, you were dangerous. It was decided to watch and learn, and to keep you limited to the poisoned lands.

"You are a breeding pair. If I let you escape into the next valley, then soon that place would be lost to us, as your children would poison it as well."

Sam Kidd felt some of his confidence slip. Any solutions that bubbled to the top of his mind were long term things, not something that would let them live once the firewood and rocks were exhausted. He was exhausted. If he only dared to take a nap....

...

The Old Man struggled to consciousness with an ill temper. There was a girl huddled in his arms, *Of course there is.* Then he spotted the balecat watching him.

What is going on here?

He quickly reviewed the memories of his sub-personalities. Sam Kidd got himself into another fix. *I could almost wish that tourist persona could learn better.*

But that was the whole point of the Kidd identity. He was a centuries-old man in a body that looked only twenty-five. He was so old and experienced that nothing could interest him, no sight could stir his awe, no girl could entice him with her charm. If he let his ancient personality run things he would be looking at suicide again quickly enough. Much better to cultivate Sam Kidd like a bonsai tree and trim off the excess when he started getting too world-weary. At least he was still living.

Checking on the Warrior's insights was disappointing. The Warrior personality gave only a twenty percent chance of killing or disabling the balecat, and no chance for the girl, as she would have to be offered as bait.

He tabled that option. The Warrior was tuned to one thing only, his personal survival. He saved the girl from the cart to keep Sam Kidd from going back for her, but that was the limit.

The Old Man at least still had enough human compassion in him to shrink from the idea of sacrificing her just yet.

I can still remember what it was like to be in love. This one seems nice. She would be good for the tourist, at least until she noticed that I don't age.

But the big cat seemed intent. Is he working the odds in that big head of his, or has he gone alpha like Earth cats watching their prey.

He forced himself to talk, remembering in a rush how to use that particular skill.

"Linguist Balecat, if I can find a solution that will keep all three of us alive, can you choose to listen, or must you follow unchanging orders from others?"

"I can listen. I do not promise anything."

The Old Man turned to the girl. He stared deeply into those wide eyes, "Listen to me, Anne. Listen carefully to my every word. Forget everything around you and listen to the sound of my words."

Tainted

Once the girl was in the trance, he stood and walked around the fire to where the balecat could look at him without strain.

"I do not live on this world, I am a traveler from many places. I know many things that you could never have heard from the villagers you study. I have a solution, but I must know more about you."

There was a deep growl from its throat. "I should kill you now. You act strangely."

"You could try," he agreed. "But then you would miss this chance to save your kind from many deaths.

"You know that we can burn whole valleys in an instant, and change the soil for all time to come. I deeply regret the deaths of the balecats. This world has too few metals in your soils for our plants to grow and we took the quick way to seed the additional metals. To you it is a poison, to us, it is a life-bringer. But we would have never done it if we had known that you were here. Your skills of secrecy were too great.

"There is a law among humans. If a native people exist on any planet, then their will must be obeyed on that world. If we had known there were people here, you could have told us to go, and we would have gone."

The cat growled, "Then go! All of you."

"The people who would have listened to that order and obeyed have already left. The villagers and the others on this world have lived their whole lives here just might ignore that law and dare to disobey. They might even choose to hide the error, by removing all balecats from this planet."

There was an angry hiss and muted roar. The Old Man could see the muscles tense in those might forelegs. He nodded as the linguist brought his natural anger under control, just as he had predicted.

"I can send your message to the right people. These farmers can be made to leave, but just as you act alone here and talk to others far distant, so do we.

"The worlds of the humans are spread far and wide, and the journey is slow. If I walk out of this valley this morning, it will be perhaps a whole generation of villagers before the new ships arrive to take them away."

The Old Man knelt down on one knee, putting his eyes on the level with the cat. He put intensity into his voice. "Whether you kill me, or let me go to send the word, remember this. You must keep your secrecy. Even if you must sacrifice another valley to the ash and poison, keep yourselves hidden!"

The balecat watched him in silence for several long minutes. "The first watcher here made many mistakes, and some others of my kind have argued to remove that error, by removing this village.

"I have chosen the risk of waiting. I have a fondness for the villagers. I have watched here for a dozen years. The one who watched before was the same way. I would regret killing them all."

The Old Man nodded, "I understand. I am a watcher of humans as well. I can understand the fondness. I look forward to the day when your kind and mine can walk together and share words and friendship. If this village dies by fang and claw, then that day will never happen."

The Old Man had one more question, "You called us tainted meat. Are we poisonous to you?"

"No, the contaminated lands refuse to grow the ved, and many other plants. Most game will not graze on the new plants. But I have heard that human meat is sweet and tasty. I have eaten many of the new animals. I quite like the mice that live in the grain fields. They have a tangy flavor. But they are so small that it is hardly worth the effort to hunt them."

The balecat looked over at the girl, "No, it is your madness that taints you. I have seen the villagers kill their own children. When I reported this, all hunts were stopped. You are a herd we must manage, but never taste."

The Old Man was hit by a rush of old memories. He put out a hand to the stone wall of the cave to steady himself. He calmed the surge of hormones with the ease of long practice.

He said, "Unfortunately, I have seen this madness before. It is a part of humans. But it can be cured."

He also looked over at the motionless girl, still in her trance, "I have an idea."

...

It took some effort, most of the daytime, to prepare the girl and the balecat, but by the time the sun was low on the horizon, Anne and Sam Kidd were out and heading down the pass, back towards the village. The hike downhill, and in the light of day was much easier than it had been coming up.

Sam smiled at Anne. She was like a big sister, and he had tremendous respect for her. He knew some of what she was planning, and he could only wish her the best.

Anne was solemn, intent on her task. She had a sense of awe, at how this insight had opened up in her mind. She knew what to do, and how. It would be hard, but her children deserved no less. She gave the stranger a brief smile, but he was soon to be gone and was really no part of her life.

They strode into the village center just at sundown, just as everyone was rushing to be indoors before dark.

Anne walked up to the big bell before the Ringerman's house. She grabbed the lever and rang peal after peal as loud as she could manage.

Doors opened all over. People stopped their rush home, and turned toward the bell.

Kidd stepped back into the shadows, out of sight.

"You!" she shouted as the Ringerman appeared. "You stand right there, and I will tell you what you need to learn."

She was an impressive figure. Her schoolteacher's dress was torn, and her face was smudged, but there was a fire in her eyes and an authority in her voice that stilled the Ringerman's first instinct to call for her capture.

"This village is a place of sorrow. Your children's blood cries out their fear and their pain. Your children's blood calls out your guilt, fresh guilt, greater than any call Irowik had on you.

"But this night! This night, the blood of your children has called me to bring an end to it!"

...

The Old Man watched from the shadows. Anne had taken the hypnotic indoctrination well. And not that it would have mattered to him, but she was primed to take this kind of geas well. If she had owned the native skill, she would have tried it on her own.

The brief dream of romance was a minor loss. The tourist could do without, and the girl would have her cause. Maybe someone would come along for her in a few years.

He looked at the tableau. She was a fire made flesh among that crowd. Many mothers and fathers were weeping openly. The Ringerman had sagged down to one knee. Many were feeling the guilt. Some had a hint of hope. It was time for the miracle.

...

She pointed an accusing finger across the crowd. "Your guilt is real, and you cannot make it go away. Only your children's blood can change it. It will change, and it will change this hour!

"Not one more drop of your children's blood will go to the balecat."

As if it was an apparition, a ghost in the shadows, the balecat roared behind her.

"Yes!" She shouted at the same instant, and her word shared an echo with the roar. With every word, the great cat took another step up behind her, until its great mass stood silently behind her like it was her own shadow.

She gave them the *new way*. Before the Old Man was half way up the road, heading back towards Port, children of all ages were scouring their homes and the fields, some for the first time in their lives out in the darkness, looking for mice to make the first offering.

Anne Lex would have her life cut out for her. She would have to change the whole culture—get them ready to face a future that might include wholesale deportation to some other new planet. She would have to change the valley into a people who kept the secret of the balecat willingly, and not out of fear.

He hoped she would enjoy the role he had programmed her to. But there was no help for it.

A wave of weariness caused him to stumble. He could feel it coming—the depression. Who was he to twist her fate? What gave him the right to overwrite her soul for his own purpose? How many more times would he do this to those who crossed his path?

He put his hand on his forehead.

He straightened up and Sam Kidd started whistling a tune, admiring the blaze of stars above as he hiked his way back toward Port.

He'd been thinking it was about time to head back toward Earth. The endless search for the Pit was likely just chasing after a fantasy. How many other people from other races had spend their lives on that same fruitless hunt?

And the lack of messages from home was disturbing. Something had happened, something he hadn't anticipated. Yes, it was better to get back to Earth and fix whatever has broken. The Pit had been a mystery for ages, that wasn't going to change. He'd come back once he'd restored communication with his organization back on Earth.

Change

Dell spoke to the sponsors of the Galactic Lens project. "I've been at this for twenty years now and I can say that I've never seen anything like it. There is definitely something out there, far from any star. It's not a black hole, and I'd bet it's not a rogue planet either. The gravitational disturbance is something planet-sized, perhaps as massive as Neptune, but I'd bet smaller. However the spectrum radiating from it is nothing like what we've seen before. Not black body. No emission lines nor absorption lines. It's definitely strange. There's a few signatures of something orbiting the place as well.

"I think it would be worth the organization's time and money to send an expedition to examine it closer."

Years ago, he would have been quaking in his boots to speak so boldly to the people who paid for his life, but he'd been through funding requests before and he'd grown a little confidence.

His eyes briefly met one of the U'tanse members and he relaxed his ineda. He'd heard that the majority of U'tanse who left the secured habitat of New Ha were tenners and didn't have telepathy anyway, but it was a gesture to show he was honest—just in case. He'd long come to peace with the idea that the majority of his U'tanse relatives could read his mind. The ineda training had helped him be comfortable living with them when he was in the Ko system.

The chairman said, "Starship flights aren't cheap."

Dell leaned forward for emphasis. "But this could very well be *new* physics. Nothing we've detected matches what our standard physics model says is possible.

"And you know very well what other things are impossible by our standard physics model as well, don't you? Tractor/pressor beams and starship leap drives. I don't think we can afford not to investigate."

He finished his presentation. It would be a month or more before they made their decision, so he had to get back to Luna to visit his family while he still could. With most of his job in rotating positions at the various Galactic Lens telescope stations, he only got back every five years or so. He wondered if Susan had waited for him like she said she would. This time he was going to invite her to come along if she'd still have him.

…

Skipping from one starship to the next, taking no scenic side-trips, it still took Sam Kidd more than four years before arriving back at the Solar system. Once the final message from his financial support team met him halfway, he switched to the Luther persona full time. He couldn't afford distractions.

His financial empire had collapsed in a disastrous meltdown when three starships arrived on Earth within six months.

One brought back fast growing protein fruit that could be cloned with just sunlight and water. The planet of origin considered them like weeds that had to be kept trimmed back, but the flesh of the fruit was a perfect match for human biology. Within two years, world agriculture was turned around, with traditional crops and meat animals quickly transitioning into the heritage market. Millions of people were living off the much cheaper and tasty Kelly Apples. The market still hadn't stabilized.

Just as humans had expanded the power of tractor/pressor beam technology to move worlds, the Prell race had adapted the TP beams in a different way, producing bubble-projectors. These bubbles could be made into instant housing, or even short-range vehicles. Starship Rome came home with a Prell prototype and a financing scheme soliciting public funding. Even low-income people could buy fractional shares in the eventual company once they reached the necessary funding level to purchase the design from the Prell. There was a frantic market in bubble shares.

One of the earliest interstellar colonies had been a Hindu isolationist group, with only one group of colonists and no creed other than the Vedas. However by the time Starship Havana passed by and radioed the surface to check on their status, the initial colony had collapsed and they were desperate for more people. They negotiated for new colonists in exchange for exclusive trade with the planet Rama. Starship Havana was advertising free transportation with no restrictions on place or origin or religion for a million new people. It quickly blossomed into a kind of lottery with many people seeking to escape their old life.

These three novel stresses on the world economy all at the same time left many investors on the wrong side of the trades, and Kidd's company was among them. Most of Kidd's money was under automated control, following schemes that had worked for him for centuries. But nothing is perfect. In the space of three days, the bulk of his wealth collapsed and his managers just walked away from it all. He was only notified because the last man out the door sent him that final report.

The spies who were monitoring Elizabeth didn't even make a final report. Their money stopped coming and they had other demands on their attention.

Luther arrived at the Cairo embarkation station with nothing more than the computer credits Sam Kidd's travel stories had earned. In spite of multiple reprints of his work over time, it wasn't much. He quickly researched the local economy and constructed an appropriate resumé for Luther Allen. He needed a job as quickly as he could.

He was desperate to immediately hunt for Elizabeth. The last report he had showed that she was following the expected path. She changed names from time to time and there had been at least three fake deaths where she walked away from one life to start another where nobody knew how old she was. He was sure he could find her, but it grated at him that he would have to wait. It would take money—and he wasn't rich anymore.

She should be passing as an adult easily by now, but his last report had her living in Copenhagen. He needed enough money to cross the Mediterranean and track her down himself. No more third party investigators who didn't really understand who they were looking for. He at least had clues. She liked to live in cities, and there was no record of her using any more sophisticated transport other than motorized scooters and bicycles. She could have always changed, but he needed to concentrate on her usual environment for now.

...

In a long abandoned mine in the Black Forest, five months later, Luther wiped the dust off his face and winched the last large stone that blocked one of his caches. So many centuries before that he'd almost forgotten it, he'd stashed gold, jewels and some pre-Plague artwork into this sealed cavity, just in case.

He'd been so rich at the time that this was nothing more than tossing a few bills under his mattress as a whim. But selling this would bring him needed cash. The gold had gone down in worth, since asteroid mining had made it more common, but even for jewels which could be synthesized, jewelry with history had worth as artwork itself.

He was familiar with buying and selling art, even though all the people he knew were long gone by now. He'd just have find the right contacts.

There were a number of such caches across the globe that he could tap, once he had enough money to travel more easily. Step by step, he needed to be wealthy again, if for no other reason than to make a good impression on Elizabeth when they met up. Likely engaging her would need the same skills he'd used in impressing all those other girlfriends over the ages. He needed to have his act together before encountering her.

...

Zealand felt old. Not much had changed since long before even he was born. The island sat as the gate between the Baltic Sea and the North Sea, with long bridges making it accessible from land even when the merfolk were at the peak of their power. The largest city, Copenhagen was a maze like all the ancient cities with none of that modern gridwork of streets like Manhattan.

Luther finally managed to track down the location of Flaskehalsen Investigations. Even though it had changed hands since the financial crisis, they still had the archives from the previous organization. He negotiated access to all the records concerning Bethe Reynolds up until their investigation ended abruptly when the bills stopped being paid.

The photo of Bethe send a shock through his system, causing a sharp pang in his chest. This was what Billie would have looked like once she grew to an apparent age of twenty. Maybe Billie wasn't really his daughter, but he'd raised her for thirty years and in spite of changing personas and another few decades of absence, the emotions hit hard.

Luther pushed those feelings back. He had a job to do.

With cash up front, he hired the spies to find her again. With their access to all the local records, they had the answer in less than a day.

Three years earlier, Bethe along with her husband and an adopted daughter had been caught in an apartment complex fire. According the news accounts, she had raced into the fire, rescuing her daughter and although her husband was injured with falling masonry, she had gone back in to help others escape, before she was trapped by the fire and burned beyond recognition.

Luther kept his reaction to himself. It was almost expected. He'd arranged his own death-by-fire several times. It was a good way to leave an old identity behind as long as you can come up with a matching corpse ahead of time. He almost admired this story. There were witnesses, so there was no doubt that the charred body was hers. The body was buried at Tuborgvej cemetery with many people attending. The news called her a hero and a saint for rescuing so many others. His only critique was the news splash with its photo of her. That would make it harder to start up a new life where no one recognizing her old identity.

The next question was where Elizabeth would have moved to. He had the records of all her earlier lives, so he spent a few days isolated in his hotel room, looking for her patterns.

Her first change, once she was old enough to be on her own was relocated two hundred kloms away. The second time, she went five hundred kloms. The third was about nine hundred. Luther pulled up a map and made a list of large cities five hundred to a thousand kloms from Copenhagen. It would be a big job, but he had a good physical description with several photos. He hurriedly contacted local investigators in each of those cities to hunt for new arrivals with matching descriptions and then he'd go check in person when there were positive matches.

Until then, he had to keep his expenses low and grow his wealth with careful management. He had so much experience with this that it only took a few hours each day.

There wasn't much he could do personally, other than tour the city. He located her husband and daughter and from a distance, they looked perfectly ordinary. He even followed them one day as they visited the gravesite at Tuborgvej cemetery. When they left he went to check on the gravesite himself.

The stone was etched with a winged angel and a simple name and dates. She had played the role of someone twenty-eight years old at the time. His mouth twisted into a smile. Nobody would have ever called Billie an angel. He wondered if he would ever tell Elizabeth about Billie.

As he was walking away from the grave, he looked back at it. Suddenly, he wondered if he should check Bethe Reynold's body. The original Beta and Billie had died. It wasn't *impossible* that the apartment fire was just as described. The death-by-fire trick required planning and preparation. She would have had to start the fire and put many other people in danger, including her family.

He could pull that off, if he had the motivation, but he'd been the hidden immortal so long that human deaths meant very little to him. She was still very young at this.

No, he had to check.

Two days later, he walked into the cemetery after sunset with a hefty walking stick, carrying a backpack. There were plenty of trees and with his excellent eyesight, he was able to work without lights.

Step one was sonic depth finder, locating the exact depth and position of the coffin. Then, he positioned the stick and began twisting. The tube extended down into the soil until it reached the top of the coffin.

With a little effort, he was able to drill a small hole in the surface of the box and force the probe down further into the body itself.

There was an endoscope with an eyepiece he fastened over his right eye. As soon as he was certain he was in the core of the body, he released a few millimeters of a chemical. Although the body was probably embalmed, there was still a difference he could check between the enzymes of normal humans and that of his, and Beta's. Normal human tissue would cause the reagent to turn pink in a five to eight seconds. His flesh would stay colorless for almost a minute.

Seconds counted off in his head. Five seconds passed with no change, then eight, then ten, fifteen. His heart was pounding and he was breathing hard by the time the first tinge of red appeared after fifty-five seconds.

The angel buried below was Elizabeth—his Elizabeth. It was the third death of Beta.

He sagged to his knees. No! No! It couldn't be.

The Old Man monitored Luther for five minutes, uncertain if the persona was strong enough for this.

But slowly, Luther got to his feet, extracted and compressed the telescoping pole and with his foot obscured the tiny hole in the soil and then he walked away.

...

Luther stayed in his Copenhagen hotel room for a month, mechanically working on his finances and each time a report arrived about some woman in one of the target cities, he carefully looked at the photos. None of them were even close to Beta. Any hope that had remained was gradually extinguished.

When Billie died, he'd changed identities and immediately went back to Isla Teresa to thaw out another frozen embryo. This time, he wondered if it would be worth it to try again.

What am I even trying to accomplish? Do I want to be the father of a new race of humanoids? We already have humans, the U'tanse, and probably a dozen Galactic races that could pass for humans on the street with just a little makeup. What's the point?

I'm so lonely. Nobody is like me.

If I want sex, companions are easy to come by. I've solved that problem.

Is it having children? Bethe Reynolds adopted a daughter, and gave up her life to save her. I raised Billie, and I can't say it was all that fulfilling.

He shook it off and went down to the street, hoping to find a restaurant that he'd never used before. He buttoned his jacket and allowed himself to appreciate the orange foliage of autumn. Closer to the waterfront, he saw a new building and the restaurant on the first floor advertised offworld cuisine.

Sam Kidd had a taste for the novel. He shifted from morose Luther to intrigued Sam and took a table. The menu advertised a few dishes he'd sampled on spaceports a hundred light years away and he was sure that the real ingredients were not to be found on Earth, but he was willing to see how close they got—squid was similar to Kwish kees after all.

Video was playing on the large display over the bar, showing some sporting event like football, but obviously in a low-gravity stadium. He could tune that out easily enough. Instead he watched the other patrons of the place. A pretty face caught his eye. It would be nice to have a companion for a while. Someone to share a meal with and to chat about inconsequential daily life. It was about time.

The food was obviously just inspired by the original kees, but it tasted fine. He was almost done when there was a news report that caught his attention.

The announcer showed a graphic of the galactic arm with a pointer.

"Researchers of the Galactic Lens project have reported that they have identified a mysterious object that some say is the source of legends all across the galaxy. Called the Pit by many alien races, this strange object isn't a star or a planet but something like a black hole—but unlike anything that astronomers have ever seen. Some speculate that strange technologies like star travel itself could have come from the Pit."

Sam abandoned his plate and pulled out his pocket computer. Among the companies he'd been investing in lately was a starship due to arrive within the month. He needed to be on it when it left.

Somebody found the Pit! I have to get there as soon as possible.

On the Butterfly Wing

The Alpine Society was one of the most well-known secret societies in the Solar system. Every three years, there was a lavish conference at the Alpine Center for Education in Stampz. Members of the Society came from all over Luna, and some from other worlds as well. Politicians and social media figures were also invited. This year, the Hurf sent a delegation to talk about education among other Galactic civilizations.

On the second day, amid the banquet and the tours to the Great Lunar Library, a few of the attendees wandered over to Fasail Memorial Center and entered the extensively soundproofed presentation center. It was time for the conference within the conference.

Teddy Barclay knew the way. He'd been at the Alpine Family meeting once before when his father brought him, when he was just twenty. He'd been the youngest one there and several people wondered if he should have been admitted. There were secrets discussed, and you had to be in on the secrets before you ever crossed the threshold.

This time he was going to be speaking, but still he was feeling the older eyes on him.

The Alpine Society was the premiere organization promoting education in the Solar system. Everybody knew about them.

The Alpine Family was only known among the members of the family and if that secret was ever exposed, the family might quickly be extinguished.

Up on the stage were the Elders, the three oldest men and the three oldest women among the family. There was a reason there were access ramps for the motorized chairs that some of them used. Even under Lunar gravity, muscles gave out with age. Unspoken was the fact that two of the actual eldest of the family had given up their position because of mental issues, but that was the reality of old age.

The Eldest of Men stood and gave a summary of the family. Their number had increased by two since the last meeting. The births and deaths were about the same, and one of the men who lived in Franklin had taken a non-family wife. She might never learn of the Alpine curse, but her children would, of necessity.

In general, members of the family were strongly encouraged to only marry within the family. The genetic curse of the Alpines would cause any who left the traditions and restrictions of the family to die out through infertility.

Another man came up on stage to cover the financial situation of the Alpine Family organization. As usual, they weren't hurting. Since the Imperial family had become Alpine generations back, money wasn't an issue.

Then Theodore Barclay's name was called and Teddy walked up to the stage.

He stared out at the group, seeing many of the people he'd considered his extended grandfathers and grandmothers while growing up. Soon enough, some of them would join the Elders.

"As you may be aware, there has been an on-going project to attempt to diagnose and hopefully cure the curse. We've known for some time that the curse was likely created as a genetic weapon, back in the time of King Thomas's War or later during the Plague. It is genetic, and my apologies for speaking of distasteful subjects, but it will probably take genetic engineering to cure us.

"We have survived through a surgical work-around, but it was never a cure. We have always hoped for a cure, but we can never tell anyone that the disease exists in the first place, so we could never get the technical help we need."

He looked over the crowd. Some were embarrassed to hear things that weren't discussed in public, others were genuinely interested in what he had to say.

"However our family isn't the only group in need of genetic assistance, so it was decided three years ago to have discussions with the U'tanse about their own needs."

He held up his hand. "Please don't ask me what the U'tanse need. They have their own secrets and I cannot divulge what I know. In simple terms, the U'tanse have never been able to easily assimilate back into the main stream of humanity, and it is suspected that their own genetic drift is the source of that problem."

Everyone knew that the U'tanse were isolated. They had a couple of colony habitats in the Solar system, but outsiders were not welcomed and the U'tanse, with few exceptions, didn't travel to the other worlds.

"As most of you know, there is an overlap between the U'tanse and the Alpine family, the Barclays. So I…" he tapped his chest, "was chosen to lead the discussions."

He gave a history of what had happened. Another of his family, his cousin Dell had brought up the possibility that there was a posible genetic engineering solution to the U'tanse isolation among the leaders on Ko. They were open to a highly restricted program to seek a genetic solution to their program, only if headed by someone with U'tanse heritage.

Secret discussions were started with the Council of Worlds special interest group that held the security codes that locked up the genetic technology. The Council was willing to help the U'tanse, but they did not want this information to be widely known.

While there were a few genetic analysis computers available in museums, no one knew whether they still worked. The Project Command was asked if the computer manufacturing machines could be programmed to produce the necessary tools, and the work was started.

"This is a very secret project and I objected to this presentation, but the Elders have the last say. In summary, I will be working in a secret facility, using this genetic engineering technology to search for the U'tanse solution and at the same time, I will be searching for a cure to the Alpine curse.

"I'll have a few years to work on this, but the instant the secret gets out, it will likely be shut down by the Council. The Council only knows about the U'tanse work, of course."

The Eldest took over. "This project will not be generally discussed, but given the significance of a possible cure to the curse, the Elders decided that the family should be informed. In the future, if Theodore Barclay makes a request, such as for blood or tissue samples, he should be accommodated with no question."

After the presentation, there were a few people who approached Teddy with their own questions. He had to turn them down.

One of his close family, his maternal grandfather, came to shake his hand. "You're the ideal person for this, you know."

"Oh?"

"Yes, part Alpine, part U'tanse, and don't forget that you're part Er Sun Kimmer on our side of the family. The Er Sun were descendants of the genetic engineers that populated the newly terraformed Luna. You've got all the right heritage for the job."

...

Three months later, Teddy stepped aboard an autoshuttle at Ceres Port.

"Computer, I haven't been informed of my destination. Where am I going?"

"According to the rules of this project, I'm unable to tell you. That said, there's nothing I can do to keep you from figuring that out on your own."

Teddy sighed. "Computer, do you understand how frustrating it is to live under so many security rules?"

"No. However, I do understand that frustration is a real thing among humans."

They left the port and the computer-controlled shuttle was in charge of the flight, but he could look at their surroundings with the display.

"I just came from Luna. Are we going back there?"

There was no response from the computer. Teddy just shook his head and watched.

Genetic engineering was so heavily restricted that most people thought it had been lost altogether. But all that information was permanently recorded in some computer somewhere and if the need was great enough—like engineering a customized raccoon for living on low-gravity Luna—then the tools and the training necessary to use them was still all there.

Nobody, however, wanted a recurrence of the Plague, or the Die-Off. Even when authorized, nobody but the people directly concerned could even know what was going on. Humans were poor at keeping secrets, so procedures kept even the humans out of the loop as much as possible.

When Teddy realized they weren't heading back to Luna, but rather an orbital position around it, he nodded to himself. They were heading for an Angel station.

Soon enough it appeared on the display, a metal butterfly covered in solar electric panels and orbiting autonomously above the Lunar atmosphere.

His heart raced. As far as he knew, no human had ever been in an Angel station. He didn't even know that they were habitable.

The autoshuttle quickly matched up with a plain, cylindrical body attached to the wings. Now, so close, they appeared enormous. Those butterfly wings stretched wider than many fields. The cylinder was dwarfed in size, and looked barely attached.

"Computer, is this habitat new?"

"Yes, it was fabricated as a stand-alone laboratory and living space."

"It doesn't look stable. It might break loose."

"That is by design. Should genetic fabrication produce something dangerous, the lab can be easily detached."

"You'd drop it into the Lunar atmosphere to burn up?" With him inside, unfortunately.

"No. There would be too much risk of contaminating the atmosphere. Remote beams would move it away from Luna and lasers would melt it down."

Teddy cleared his throat. "Yes. I see. That's a more tidy solution."

The shuttle's airlock latched with the lab and he stood up. "Is the lab habitable yet?"

"Yes. Pre-warming began when we left Ceres. You can move your things over immediately."

...

The shuttle left immediately, but the computer's voice in the lab was the same.

Teddy said, "If I'm going to be living here alone for a while, I'm probably going to be talking to you, just for the sake of hearing another voice. I'm not supposed to be making any contact with people at home."

"This was expected. This computer has been loaded with a casual interaction system that allows me to make stream-lined determination of what is an actual order and what is smalltalk."

Teddy nodded. He didn't expect much. Like everyone else, he'd chatted with a computer until he was confident it was just a simple question and answer machine, not another person.

He wished Debbie had survived. He had married young, but before they even had children she was lost in a flood. Maybe he wouldn't have brought her along on this project, but it would have been nice to have her with him.

"I guess I'd better get started with my training."

The display that had been showing the view of the Angel station with Luna's clouds in the background immediately switched to text and diagrams.

"I wish I had real windows."

"I understand, but if there were windows, remote observers might be able to look inside the lab, and that's prohibited."

He sighed. "Give me a summary of what you are displaying."

. . .

When he was young, Teddy had thought he might become a medical doctor, but two things derailed that ambition. The first was his encounter with a healer from the U'tanse. There was nothing more discouraging than realizing that he lacked the basic senses that made for a truly great healer. When he learned the U'tanse secret—that there were psychic senses that, while useful, also kept them isolated from the rest of humanity—he knew it was a barrier he could never overcome.

The other barrier was ignorance. The technical knowledge of how the human body worked was deliberately locked away behind the anti-genetic rules. He couldn't even become the best non-psychic doctor because of the reaction to past mistakes.

Now, however, he was drinking in all this forbidden knowledge and he was starting to feel the effects of long hours with nobody to tell him to take a break.

"Computer, I need you to monitor my diet and sleep."

"Shall I blank the screens when you reach your limits?"

"No, don't go that far. Just remind me."

"Then you should stop now, eat and sleep."

Teddy nodded. "I think you're right."

. . .

The genetic analyzers and other tools were pretty straightforward. He tried them out by feeding his own spit into a vial and letting the machine produce his full genetic code. It was when he tried comparing his code with a standard-human code that he was overwhelmed by the data. There were so many differences and he couldn't tell what was minor and what might be the needed clue to the Alpine curse.

The computer had suggestions. "You shouldn't compare your code with that standard. The built-in model human code is centuries old and was probably imperfect even back then. You should compare closely related current samples with the desired difference."

Teddy had made sure that the computer could keep any of his secrets. Not even the Council of Worlds could override the code and find out what he was doing.

"So, for the U'tanse, I should get samples from two siblings—one a telepath and the other a tenner?"

"Yes."

"And for the Alpines?"

"It's not that easy. There are no Alpine siblings without the curse."

Teddy sighed, "I guess I'll just have to get samples from more distantly related families in Stampz. Non-Alpine families. Otherwise this is going to be impossible."

The computer said, "It has been done before."

Source of the Curse

"What do you mean, it's been done before?"

The computer said, "Back at the time of the Plague, on Alexandria, a traveling doctor analyzed the genetic code of the people there, the ancestors of the Alpines, and discovered the variation. She created the surgical treatment that allowed females to regain fertility."

Teddy remembered the story his wife told him on their wedding night. The story was the same.

"How did you know this?" It was supposed to be a closely guarded secret among the Alpine family.

"All person-to-person communications via computer messaging is always encrypted, however when a computer is monitoring speech, awaiting orders, that information is not inherently secured. Over the years, this story has been told several times among people in the presence of an open microphone.

"Normally, this type of information isn't easily searchable, but I was given the order to index and collect any background information related to the project, and these conversations were considered relevant."

Teddy paused a moment. "So anyone could ask another computer to relay things I'm saying here in this lab?"

"No. This project is under strong security and nothing is available to outsiders."

Teddy took a deep breath. *I'm going to have to have a talk with the Elders when I get back. People are too casual about having a computer with them all the time.*

"Back to your original statement. You said that doctor used genetic analysis to discover the Alpine curse. I thought tools like that were banned by then."

"Yes, but not only did she discover the curse, but she also diagnosed the Plague. She was perhaps the first person to send out an alert about its hazards. She couldn't have done that without the proper tools. It may have been a bootleg machine. There is no record of her possessing a genetic analyzer."

Teddy leaned forward, "Then can we access that data and use her analysis?"

"There is no record of it. It is likely that it was on the Darnell Farms habitat when it was destroyed during the Plague. At that time, communications were overwhelmed and there was no chance to relay that data to another computer."

"Is there anything else in your background research that I could use to help my analysis?"

"Records from that traveling doctor are limited. Records from the person who created the curse are suspiciously absent. It is likely that he used isolated computers for his work that never connected to the network."

Teddy felt a shock. "So, you know who created the Alpine curse? Was it just one person? Perhaps we could research him?"

"That request has reached my ethical barrier. The information exists, but I cannot release it to you."

"Why?"

"The stability of society is based in part on secrets."

Teddy sighed. The Alpines knew it well. Without secrets, they would be hunted down and killed—every man, woman, and child. The U'tanse had secrets as well. If the computer had to play it fair, then he had to accept that there were secrets that couldn't be released.

"Okay, then please research everything that you know of this person and look for any clue to the curse that might have been accidentally released. Anything could be useful."

...

It took a month to get samples from the U'tanse. He had three pairs of tissue samples of close siblings, one of each was a tenner with no telepathy and the other was a normal telepathic U'tanse.

Teddy was deep in his analysis of the results, finding common differences and matching them to known genetic traits in the database, when the computer interrupted him.

"I have the data you requested."

"Which data? I've asked you for hundreds of things."

"I have restricted information from the creator of the Alpine curse."

He instantly forgot the charts he'd been searching all day long.

He whispered, "Tell me what you know."

"The creator of your genetic disease was captured and dosed with a truth drug while his computers were nearby listening. For a brief time, he bragged of what he'd done, and how, and why. None of this was locked down by his privacy commands because they had been deactivated by his captor. I have this recording. Do you wish me to play it?"

"Yes."

"This was recorded during the outbreak of the Plague. Voices begin with the moment Paula Campbell shot a chemical dart at her captor, true name unknown:

There was a shout, then a man's voice said, "A truth drug. Right."
He laughed. "It won't do you any good. You don't think I know how
to handle my own poisons? I made them all."

Paula said, "So why are you fighting, if they can't hurt you?"

"I didn't say they wouldn't hurt … s' just won't do you any good.
You've already got the fever."

"Tell me about the fever."

"You can't make me. I can resist this … stuff."

"But you do know about it?"

"Of course I do. I made it. It is mine."

"You engineered the disease?"

"Ya. Custom virus. S'most sophis. Ticated. Got my tongue."

"Why? You're killing people by the thousands!"

"Millions." The words were slowing as he struggled to pronounce
them correctly. "It is for humanity's own good. You can't handle too
much technology."

"You can't do that! What gives you the right?"

Teddy had to shift his thoughts. The speaker wasn't talking about the Alpine curse. He was talking about the Plague itself! This was the creator of the worst disease in human history—the greatest mass-murderer in all history. He gripped the armrest on his chair.

He had to listen to every word as this monster described what he'd done, giving the woman his careful justifications for wiping out the bulk of humanity in order to remove mankind's ability to create world-threatening technologies.

She argued with him, rejecting the idea that killing people was good for them.

Just when they started arguing about the word "genocide", did he tense up.

"And I know what I am talking about. I've done genocide, and I know the difference."

"What?"

"Genocide. I destroyed a gene line. People, if that makes it any clearer."

"Who? Why?"

His voice showed anger. "A little history. Life Force Technologies was a contract house in Australia. That kingdom was going to try to leapfrog northern technology by building custom plants and animals. They had grown blimps, better crops, and whole new sea creatures. They would control the land, sea, and air before the northerners could invent something better.

"Among other projects, Life Force got the contract to design a human gene structure without radiation sensitivity.

"Life Force thought to tackle the cancer problem by removing all unnecessary DNA. They re-wrote the genes with none of the booby traps and dead-ends that evolution had left in the chromosomes. That, with a careful choice of metabolism to naturally clean out free-radical ions and other simple radiation damage poisons, would have completed the job.

"Of course, since their contract was cost-plus, they had no incentive to stop there. As long as they had a clean slate to create a new type of human, they went all the way. Like I said. I have the best of everything human. Every genetic virtue I have came from some human, somewhere.

"*Then, some bright bio-engineer had the idea to tweak with lon-gevity. After all, death is just nature's way of controlling cancer. Cells die when their genetic timer runs out. That way, most damaged cells grow a tiny little tumor, and then die out on their own.*

"*But since they had removed most cancer causes in the genetic cleanup, why not do away with the expiration date?*

"*And so they did. But that had side effects, like cartilage growth and overall maturity. They had to tweak a few hormonal settings. Nothing major.*

"*Just enough to leave me an apparent child of ten when I was thirty years old! When I was still a toddler, the Die-Off happened. And then the witch-hunts.*

"*Life Force dumped me in a foster home, with barely enough cover story to hide my origin. The company knew they were targets. They picked up en masse and went into hiding. First, it was a little farm village in Tasmania, but when their cover was blown, they moved again. By the time space habitats were being built, they moved to space, where they could hide out until the anti-genetic hysteria died out.*

"*Well, by the time I had come into my independence, all the com-puter records were long gone. Still, I found a paper trail and tracked them down. They were still there, living as one tribe, still hiding in space.*

"*I bided my time. They weren't going anywhere. I had time to plan my vengeance.*"

The man went on a tirade, explaining his childhood pain and explain-ing that his genetic code was so incompatible with humans that he could never have children.

And then came the critical moment.

"*So, what did you do to them?*" she asked.

"*Justice! I crafted the perfect penalty. Their sin was genetic craft-ing. I gene-crafted them a disease. They ran and hid away. I hid their disease. They made me sterile. I made them sterile. A critical sequence in the disease is a direct copy of part of one of my chromosomes. In a sense, they helped design the code that wiped them out.*

"*Oh no, I didn't kill anyone. Instead I doctored their medical supplies with a mobile genetic splice that had no symptoms at all. It just insured that they would have no grandchildren. Simple as that. A hundred years ago, the initial infection got half of them. It is sexually transmitted, so normal marriages and a little fooling around would soon get them all. I haven't checked lately, but I wouldn't be a bit surprised if there's nothing left but some old remnants, wondering why they never had grandkids.*

"Now, that is genocide! You don't even have to bloody your hands to do it right."

"Monster."

When the recording ended, Teddy was convinced. Everything matched. His ancestors had been the creators of this artificial man and he had tried to wipe them out with the curse!

Ethical Decisions

"Computer, I need to discuss this with the Elders."

"There are restrictions."

Teddy was content that it wasn't an abrupt denial. The computer explained the problems.

He was still restricted to the lab for the initial three-year period, so he couldn't go down to Luna. It would have to be a video meeting. In addition, no one should be able to infer the location of the genetics lab, so speed-of-light delay on the video needed to be disguised.

Teddy made the case that the Elders needed to hear the audio recording for themselves. So much history of the Alpine family that had been hidden for centuries has now been revealed, as was the relationship between the family and the person who created the curse.

Computer had its concerns, but they worked it out. Teddy sent a text message to the Elders. It was set up, even though one of them was in Franklin.

"Strict secrecy is necessary. Soundproofed rooms are required."

Three days later, Teddy stared at five of the Elders in a Stampz conference room and one who was obviously sitting in a closet with clothes hanging behind him.

Teddy made his greetings, re-emphasized the security warnings and explained the situation. "The person who created the Alpine curse has been discovered, but so much more has also been uncovered. I need to play an audio recording."

As he answered questions, it was plain that the computer had added a eight-second delay in the transmissions, as if he were in a remote habitat even farther away than the Lagrangian stations. It wasn't even worth a comment. All of the Elders had experience with distant communications over their long lives.

Teddy explained the situation. The recording made centuries ago was during a brief lapse of the man's security when he was attacked and captured.

The Eldest of Women raised her hand and he paused his explanations.

"Does this mean the computers are recording everything we're saying?"

"As it was explained to me, person-to-person talks, like this one, are secured, but if you were to be chatting with a family member at home and there was a computer listening for commands, the unrelated conversations could be recorded.

"Normally, nobody will ever find those recordings and listen to them, but the possibility exists—unless the computer is ordered to secure any such conversations."

The Elders immediately began discussing how to begin to secure everything. Teddy raised his hand.

"I am pleased that the Elders are taking this security issue seriously, but this issue is minor compared to the audio you need to hear. May I proceed?"

They agreed to work on the security problem afterward.

Teddy set the stage, and played the recording. The faces of the Elders were fascinating to watch. There was horror and shock and even sadness.

When the recording was over, the first question came from one of the women. "The monster, he implied that he was very long-lived. Just how long did he live?"

"The computer has said that he might still be alive today."

Another Elder asked, "It is implied that if you could get a tissue sample of this man, then you might be able to decode the curse and block it. Is that correct?"

"That is my prime focus. If I could get his genetic code then I could compare it to ours and find all the places where it matched. That would narrow down the search for the curse and hopefully give clues on how to deactivate it."

"Then we should try to track him down immediately."

The Eldest of Men said, "There is an issue. Will he agree to this?"

One of the women, wearing a cap over her thinning gray hair said, "Of course we need the sample. Does it matter if he agrees?"

"Would you agree to give up a sample of your genetic code if, say the Council of Worlds asked for it? Would you put your children at risk?"

The guy in Franklin said, "But he's a monster. He created the Plague. He's a criminal. Does he even have rights?"

The Eldest of Men shook his head. "Isn't his criminal past just an excuse to do what we want with him, regardless of what he wants?

"We have to face the reality that we, our ancestors, created this monster. Regardless of their intent, they chose to protect their family and by discarding him, made him into a monster in the first place.

"We bear part of the guilt for the Plague, and maybe we earned the curse, by taking the easy way out. I'm not going to agree to ignore the side-effects again. Whatever we choose to do, let's think this out and take the ethical route."

"But my child is innocent."

Teddy was glad he wasn't part of that group. He was just a worker, following their orders. But he texted a private question to the computer. Then he held up his hand.

The Eldest asked, "Theodore, you have a comment?"

"The computer says that the person who created the curse is likely still alive, but has taken a starship out of the Solar system some time back. The computer does not know where he is."

"Does that mean that we have to wait, perhaps years, for him to return? If so, then is this debate just a fruitless exercise?"

"The ethical issue still exists. How are we going to deal with this person when the time comes?"

"What do we make of the fact that he's still alive after centuries? Is this something we could apply to regular humans?"

It was a few minutes after Teddy explained in simple terms how the longevity worked and gave them no hope that it could be used for others, when the computer texted him.

Teddy read the lengthy message, his heart pounding. He raised his hand again.

"Theodore?"

"The computer has done some more research. The ethical issue may have changed.

"There were two artificial persons created by Life Force Technologies—a male and a female. The female was killed during the Plague when her habitat crashed into Ceres. The male recovered her body once the Earth's embargo was lifted, and using genetic technology, managed to create new embryos to be raised to adulthood.

"The man has had bad luck with his restoration project and both of his clone attempts have died. One was burned, but one is buried in Copenhagen on Earth.

"However, there is a significant issue with the first of them, the original. She was the doctor who discovered the curse and gave us the surgical treatment. It was shortly after that, on a different habitat, that the Plague happened and she was killed."

There was more silence than just the speed-of-light delay as the Elders absorbed this new information.

The Eldest of Women said, "We have revered this doctor from the beginning. It's unbelievable that she's the same kind of… person that created the Plague."

The man in the closet said, "Not so unbelievable. If there were two super geniuses, living independently of each other back then, and one was smart enough to create the curse, it's not surprising that the other was smart enough to decode it."

The Eldest of Men said, "Theodore, we will be discussing this for some time to come. You don't need to listen to all of this. We'll contact you. We may have to set up another meeting, but this isn't something we can decide in a few minutes."

...

Teddy knew what he would do, if he were in charge. He'd locate that gravesite in Copenhagen and do enough digging to get a good tissue sample. After that, it would just be a lot of database work to locate the code that caused the curse.

He was expecting a call from the Elders to get more details about that grave and the person who she had been. Certainly he was still stuck at the lab for now, but there were others who could handle Earth's gravity and deal with the process of disinterring the body. All he needed was the tissue sample.

When the call from the Elders came, he had the information ready.

"Theodore, the decision of the Elders is that any tissue sample has to be given with the consent of the owner."

"What? But ... he's somewhere out of the system and out of contact. I'd thought using the sample from the grave would be acceptable."

"I understand your thinking, and we did consider that, but the revelation that an ethical shortcut by our ancestors contributed to the Plague and the Alpine curse is too strong a signal that we can't do the same ourselves. It's harder this way. More Alpine children are at risk.

"However, we're going to take the high road. That means two courses of action.

"One, we'll send a message via standard computer to that missing person and just hope that we can make our case."

"That will be hard, considering that we can't reveal the curse."

"Indeed. So we're also going to also proceed with the second option. We're going to try to get permission from the female."

"Ah ... how?"

"Didn't you say that he created embryos of the female from the original and grew two of them to adulthood? Isn't it reasonable that somewhere in his genetic laboratory there might be another preserved embryo?

"It was the suggestion of the Eldest of Women that we owed that original doctor who preserved our line the opportunity to be brought back to life herself. We need to find that laboratory and raise a new version of her, and when she's an adult, we'll ask her for permission to use her sample."

Teddy was shocked. "I ... I guess that's possible. It will take some time—decades."

"Yes, we'll all be gone by then and it will be up to the next generation of Elders to follow through with this. You might be the only one left who's been in this from the beginning."

Teddy put his hand on his forehead. "I guess I need to get the computer to help us locate the place. I assume you'd raise the new one on Luna?"

"Yes, under the wing of the Alpines. The slow development might be a problem and we're the right organization for this. Our ancestors should have done the same with the original pair."

"Okay then, I'll contact you when I get any information. You're aware I'm stuck here in the lab. Someone else will have to do the fieldwork on Earth."

"That's fine. We've been extending our reach all over the Solar system. We have people on Earth."

After the call ended, Teddy asked the computer, "Do you know where the immortal had his lab on Earth? I assume you overheard that last call."

"Yes, I heard. And yes, I do know where the Earth laboratory is. The issue is whether I can divulge that information."

"I guess you have your secrecy guidelines. I'm asking you to recheck everything and make sure. This is an important step in searching for the cure for the curse. A lot of people will be depending on it."

"I will search that information."

Teddy sighed. Maybe it would work out, maybe not. He wasn't at all sure about this plan to reclone the female. It seemed sketchy. Were the Elders doing it for the cure, or was it just to pay back some debt to the original doctor?

"I'm glad I'm just a tech," he mumbled.

...

It was less than a day when the computer provided the answer.

"Isla Teresa? Where is that?"

"On the Pacific coast of South America. It is an underground facility and the doors have been secured. Digging may be required."

"I'm glad you are able to provide the information."

"It was a close decision. Rechecking the primary records showed that the immortal neglected to use his usual security procedures around the time the first clone died. Perhaps he was distracted.

"Even then, only you, acting under the authority of this Council-approved project have sufficient priority to request such a search."

Teddy smiled, "So it was an ethical decision for you as well."

"Yes. Don't expect to be able to extend such searches in the future."

He nodded. "I'm content. Breaking through his privacy means someone else could break through mine.

"I'll pass on the details to the Elders."

The Call of the Pit

Luther Allen looked out the window from the dining area of Station E-1, permanently oriented to view the Pit. He could barely see E-2 and N-1 also in orbit around the object. There were several Earth-owned stations around the Pit, and three from other races as well.

When it was first discovered by the research vessel sent by Galactic Lens, it had triggered something like a gold rush mindset.

The Pit was not a planet. The faint blue globe was just a static atmosphere that had collected at the neck of an Einstein-Rosen bridge. Every probe that had been sent through failed.

Analysis of the rubble that orbited the Pit was an eye-opener. Some of it had been formed on the other side and showed that physics over there was entirely different.

The speculation that the impossible inventions of tractor/pressor beams and leap technology had somehow come from this other universe was confirmed when some of the orbiting rubble contained the crystals that were the key component of TP projectors.

The Puana, the inventors of TP technology, formally admitted that they were only able to create it from those crystals that they had discovered drifting in interstellar space long ago. The Galactics debated for four years over whether the discovery of these crystals here meant that TP technology was to be downgraded from type-2 to type-1, but considering that there were just a small dusting of the crystals, the Puana retained the more valuable type-2 classification for their invention.

The Click, the owner of starship drive technology wasn't admitting anything, but both those species lived in systems within a few dozen lightyears of the Pit. It was clear that at least those two impossible technologies were sourced from material that had come from the Pit.

Every bit of material near the Pit was being taken apart and examined in detail, in hopes that there would be new magical materials of unimaginable use. The huge expense of moving a science station into the Pit's orbit was seen as just table stakes. No one could discover any cross-universe samples without being there, searching the vacuum constantly.

Two science stations had been destroyed in the process. While some alien material had crystallized into a stable form, some was not so stable, no longer able to hold onto its native physical laws. Evaporating caused some of it to explode as the "atoms" reverted to primordial energy.

Luther worked as a researcher on one of the surviving stations. He'd been at it since he'd arrived, just two years after the discovery.

Callahan has commented on my appearance twice now. Who knows how many others have noticed that I'm not aging like the others of my team?

Sooner or later, he'd have to 'die' and come back in another identity. The problem here was that the science community was so small that he couldn't come back as another scientist here. He'd be recognized.

A new starship arrived from Earth, and everybody received notices on their computers of messages from home. Luther was a little surprised that he received one as well.

He just glanced at the text. It was some organization on Luna that wanted to talk with him. He deleted it. Nobody on Luna had any idea who he was. They'd probably just located his name on a list somewhere and he had no interest in making a trip back to the Solar system just to give a speech on the Pit.

...

Teddy Barclay was grateful for the gravity suit, basically a skintight undergarment that allowed low-gravity people like him to exist comfortably on high gravity worlds. Not that the moon of Ha was high gravity, but all the inhabited areas were kept at roughly one gravity. His ancestor, Ohen bar Clay had grown up here, and Teddy had scheduled a family visit with relatives, once he was through with his primary business.

The initial work had been completed on the tenner drug. He just needed to present to the Restoration Committee and get their approval. Unless there was some kind of last minute problem, he would turn it over to them and hopefully it would smooth out the U'tanse emigration to the Solar system.

He remembered the last time he'd visited the Elders on Luna, each time it seemed like there were new faces and the older ones died or retired. This group of U'tanse felt similar, even though they were much younger.

Teddy gave his technical summary, thanked the group for their support in getting tissue samples over the years, and outlined what he expected to happen.

"It's pretty straightforward. Should anyone want to migrate to the Solar system permanently, then to preserve the U'tanse secret, they should take this drug and all their children will be tenners. Only the psychic trait would be affected."

The committee had been following his annual reports and they mostly understood. A white-haired healer was particularly interested in the DNA and the complex of genes that turned the psychic gifts on and off. Teddy was prepared with charts.

"It looks like it is a combination that wouldn't occur frequently," she said. "It's obviously the DNA bottleneck and our reinforcement that has made it ubiquitous among the U'tanse."

One man asked, "Could this drug be made airborne?"

Teddy frowned. It was always conceived as an injectable treatment. "I don't know. Why?"

"I was just thinking about the hivers. Maybe we could send a robotic probe and dose the whole colony and cure the whole hive at once."

Teddy knew just a little of the history of the hivers. Supposedly there were three isolated colonies, two on planets and one in a self-sustaining habitat. All were under strong blockades, since anyone who might visit could be easily converted into a member of the hive by their strong psychic force.

Teddy was a little upset. "That sounds like a weapon. They certainly wouldn't agree to it. Besides that's not how this works. Taking the drug doesn't remove your own telepathy. That's dependent on brain structures that have already been trained. It would just make their new infants tenner by birth. Don't we have records that hivers can convert the non-telepathic by force? It wouldn't change them. It certainly wouldn't cure the hive when they can just fix their own children."

Another member waved his hand. "And think how disruptive such a weapon would be to ordinary U'tanse culture. We depend on our gifts to live our day to day life. Better not let an airborne version ever be invented! I can see it used against us one day."

Teddy said, "On that issue, all the information about the project and the design and creation of the drug itself are included in the materials I've brought with me. The Council of Worlds which permitted the genetic engineering in the first place would not allow any of the genetic sequencers to leave the restricted lab, so the drug is designed to be grown via ordinary viral techniques under your control.

"The actual data at the lab is under a tight security lock and no one has access to it. If it turns out that you need changes made, I'll have to personally unlock it to reactivate the program."

He shrugged. "I had a nightmare that there might be a human-U'tanse war someday and this information might be used against us, so I made sure that could never happen."

The healer chuckled. "Maybe we should tempt you to stay here on Ha with us."

He smiled. "Unfortunately, I have other projects I have to get back to. I love this opportunity to come visit my ancestor's home, but I have a family waiting for me back on Luna."

He hoped his ineda was good enough to block all the information about the Alpine curse, but he couldn't help but visualize his unique granddaughter. He had a life-long project still ahead of him.

...

Bethany and her friend Sue hiked to the heavy house regularly. It was hardly a twenty-minute walk from either of their places. Bethany was so glad to have her as a school friend, and it hadn't taken much argument to get the girl to come along with her. Bethany had dreams of traveling the worlds someday and infected Sue with some of that ambition. Anyone who wanted to live on Earth without a wheelchair needed regular exercise under heavy gravity.

"Do you think it's Earth day, or Mars day?" asked Sue with a little hesitancy.

"I'm pretty sure it's Earth day. Don't you remember we played football last time, and they only do that on Mars day?"

Sue sighed. "It's all too heavy for me. I don't know why you're so anxious to get those muscles. Being able to travel is still years away."

Bethany shook her head. "No, we've got to get our bodies trained now, while they're still flexible enough to adapt." Although in her case, she did have lots of time, but Sue was only thirteen and her teenage years would be over in a flash. They could only be friends for another year or so and then Bethany would have to go live with Grandpa Teddy and Grandma Aster for a couple of years again. Then she'd get to pick another Mom and Dad for a few years.

She'd lived in Stampz, Franklin, and Condorcet, all with Alpine families. Her new parents would know her secret but she had to pretend to be her apparent age. It wasn't a bad life, and she enjoyed her teen friends, even though she was fast approaching forty herself.

It had been two decades earlier when she had learned the full truth about herself. She'd even read the details of her previous lives, at least the parts of them that the computer had been able to discover.

Those weren't me. But I could still make all the same mistakes.

The idea of past lovers was tempered by the stories of past betrayals. The other Betas had husbands and adopted children, joys and tragedies. The same could happen to her as well.

And then, there was Alpha. It was disturbing that the only time they had been together, she'd killed herself to get away from him.

The only person in the universe like me and he's a monster.

She smiled to herself. *But supposedly I'm a saint. I wonder if I can get through my teenage years without falling for some unsuitable guy.*

Sue asked, "What are you thinking about? You've got a funny look on your face."

Bethany grinned. "Guys, what else. Is David still hanging around you?"

"Why? Are you interested?"

"Maybe, but I'm never going to do anything about it. I've got my plans."

Sue gave an exasperated sigh. "Yeah, going to college on Earth. Oxbow or someplace."

"Oxford. It's famous, one of the oldest schools in the Solar system."

Her real plans didn't include any college, it would be a waste of time, but Oxford made a handy story she could pull out anytime to excuse her passion for gravity exercises or a reason for ignoring a good-looking boy. She couldn't play the saint among her friends. They knew better.

. . .

Years later Bethany watched the World Tree under the Ceres Dome as her shuttle pulled away, heading for her destination. She was sad to see it dwindle to just a green dot on the globe. Her multi-world tour had included several places on Earth where earlier incarnations of her had lived. Visiting the grave of Bethe Reynolds was positively spooky, knowing another her was just under the ground. She liked the gravestone with the angel.

She had also visited the Library of Alexandria with a special permit from the Alpine Society. It had been fascinating to browse the shelves wearing an oxygen mask.

Mars had been on her wishlist, but she couldn't make that work. She had a different priority to deal with.

Once she reached an adult appearance without makeup, the Elders finally made the formal request to use her tissue sample in their delayed hunt for a cure for the Alpine curse.

Although she wasn't really a member of the Alpine family, she'd lived as one for so many years that she'd discovered the secret of the curse on her own. Later, when she'd listened to Alpha's audio recording where he bragged about wiping out the people who had created them, she quickly understood that the Elders of the Alpines hadn't funded her life just on a whim.

She was grateful they hadn't pressured her into giving her permission back when she was young and dependent. It gave her time to consider all the options, and to make her plans.

This tour was just one step in a grander scheme. She just hoped Grandfather wouldn't be too disappointed in her.

. . .

"Professor Barclay!" The call came from his left, as Teddy sat on the bench near the Stampz Airport landing area.

It was just one of his students. He waved back, smiling. He probably only had a couple of more years left at the university. The Elders had sent him a notice that he was on their list to be added when one of the men retired. It wasn't compulsory service, but there was a lot of tradition involved and he'd have a lot of explaining to do if he turned it down.

Not that being in the group scared him particularly, he'd been working with the Elders for more years than he'd care to count.

He was still working for them, in a way. Bethany was due to arrive back from her grand tour and he looked forward to seeing her. It was strange to see her every time she came back to live with her grandparents between families.

She was so perpetually young, especially when he could compare her with his own children, now getting gray hair on their own. Sadly, Aster was no longer with him there to greet her. Maybe the grandfather story had started as just a fiction, as Bethany needed the stability of a permanent family, even as she lived with temporary foster parents for a few years at a time.

But now, he couldn't think of her as anything but his own granddaughter. He glanced at the wall clock, waiting for her flight.

But his pocket computer caught his attention. He frowned. It was a message from her.

I'm sorry Grandfather. But I won't be on the flight to Stampz. I have other plans. I've thought about this for years. I owe everything to you and the Alpines. You brought me to life, after all.

But, sadly, you taught me to think for myself, and to make my own moral judgements. If that man had died, then I would give you the permission to use my DNA code with no reservations.

But he's not dead. And this whole problem hinges on his existence— his history and the ancestors of the Alpines that made him.

I owe it to myself to hear his side of it, from his own mouth, on my own, far from the eyes of my families.

So, by the time you receive this message, I will have already joined the crew of Starship London and I'm heading for the Pit. Don't try to stop me, and certainly don't worry about me. I've been planning this for four years now and I'm sorry for hiding all my schemes from you.

Should I not achieve what I need to confirm in the next five years, an automated message will arrive giving the Elders the permission to use my code. I know you already have a sample in cold storage.

My only regret is not coming to say goodbye in person. But hopefully, I'll return soon. I just need to do this alone.

Teddy blinked away some unexpected tears. It was a little bit of a shock, but it was exactly what his Bethany would do. He just prayed she would be safe, going to confront the most dangerous monster in human history.

Gina's Arrival

I'm Gina Parker. She nodded as the starship leaped the fifty-plus light-years from her last destination. She wouldn't be Bethany again until this was done. *All my other incarnations were probably better at swapping identities than me.* She'd had varying last names over the years but she'd always been Bethany or Beth. Changing cities and having a family everywhere to protect her had given her enough confidence that no one would connect the various lives together.

That wasn't good enough this time. She'd made her first jump from the Solar system to the Ba system with a supply run for the U'tanse base that was in orbit around the super-earth water world of Ba. Down below, the flat, turtle-like inhabitants traded various shelled-fish in exchange for human poetry. It was a relationship based more on their shared history than on economics, but the U'tanse and the Ba had a long-term view of their alliance.

She had marveled at the giant world she'd probably never land on, not that there was much more than a few islands that could support a landing craft. Humans couldn't stay there without protective gravity suits and strong cancelling floor gravity. Listening to the workers who managed the lifting of the cargo containers, it was unlikely Ba could ever have a real valuable commodity to trade that could pay for the energy necessary to lift it off their world. Most of the money involved came out of the U'tanse diplomatic budget. The decorative shells were destined for the Uuaa who carved them into artwork.

Bethany became B. Parker, and then G. B. Parker, and then Gina Parker over four leaps between systems, changing jobs as she went, finally stepping into a prepared identity designed for her work at the Pit.

"Parker, report to shuttle A."

It was time. She hefted her travel bag and strolled down the corridor to the shuttle bays. She paused at an exterior display currently showing the Pit as a faint blue disk. The starship couldn't get any closer. The rules for the Pit system were very strict. Leap engines couldn't be deployed close to the bridge between universes. TP beams couldn't be aimed at it either. Nobody knew the real physics in play here, so when the Galactic Lens established the rules, they were very cautious in setting their limits.

A TP-powered shuttle would transfer the cargo and the occasional passenger to the Pit Warehouse, itself in orbit ten million kloms from the Pit. The research stations were closer, but cargo could only be delivered to the Warehouse. Smaller, low power shuttles were used by the research stations to move things within the system.

She tapped the controls to turn the display into a large mirror, just to double-check her disguise—strong red hair, good for at least a month before she had to fix it up. Dark brown eyes, probably good for six months. Skin that made her look like she was in her late twenties.

She hardly looked at all like the Bethany of her younger years, but it still might not be enough. Alpha had raised her earlier incarnation for years, after all. There was a limit to what she could change. Makeup could help, but he could probably recognize that as well.

Gina really needed to observe him before he recognized her as Beta. From her research, she knew he had charmed many women and he had a strong incentive to charm her as well.

Once on the shuttle, she ignored the pilot's looks. She knew she looked unkempt, as if she'd been up all night. It was one of her standard tricks to discourage conversation. On the starships, the male-to-female ratio was still heavily skewed and she didn't want to be considered fresh meat. She could quickly reverse the look when she arrived at her destination. For the interviews, she'd need to look professional.

Watching the exterior view as they traveled, it gave her a much better feel for the size of the Pit system—a planetary-sized system rather than a star system. The Pit itself had no real surface, just a gravitationally bound gas cloud, but everything was in orbit around it, as if it were a planet and the stations were its moons. There were no stars within five light years, so stations were dark except for navigation lights. The Pit had a glow, but it was hardly in the same class as sunlight.

Warehouse was built on a rogue asteroid that Galactic Lens had located and steered into its orbit over a ten-year period. It had to be massive to give the shuttles something to latch onto for in-system transport.

She was both excited to be approaching the stage where she would play her role, and a little guilty for denying the Alpines her permission to use her genetic sample. The Alpines had to have been frustrated at her decision, and she was grateful so few of them knew she existed. The disease that had plagued their families for hundreds of years might be cured, and she was holding back the critical clue. They had certainly tried on their own.

They had gutted the Isla Teresa laboratory and smuggled the banned equipment to a remote crater on Luna, training their own geneticists in secret. Still, there was a limit to what they had been able to accomplish. A handful of scientists couldn't hope to duplicate a whole branch of science that peaked so very long ago, and then had been deliberately wiped out.

After a quick visit to the restroom to clean herself up, Gina checked in through the immigration office on Warehouse. Earth owned the Pit by right of discovery and they controlled entry to the Pit system.

However, from the very beginning, the Galactic Lens researchers knew they would have to tread lightly. Humanity was a very young race among the Galactics. Trying to hog this major discovery entirely would likely turn the community against them, so even as humans struggled to gain new technologies from the Pit they also leased the right for other races to make their own efforts. Even if an alien race discovered something amazing, humanity would get a percentage.

Still, Solar system officials monitored every starship that arrived and enforced the rules. Gina's records had arrived on an earlier ship so they were ready for her. The actual job interview had taken place on Earth.

There was a man standing outside the immigration office. "Parker?"

"Yes." She looked at him carefully. He was about the right height for Alpha, but he looked out of shape and a bit overweight. Never in all her years had she gained weight no matter how she ate. Her metabolism and her natural inclination to exercise kept her body right in the proper zone even when she gorged. Alpha would be the same. This wasn't him.

"I'm Douglas Trane. You'll be working in my department. They sent me over to pick you up and welcome you to Pendulum." He had a polite smile.

She stepped closer. "I'm so glad to meet you! I have so many questions about the work here."

He glanced away toward the corridor marked D. "We'll talk on the way. First we've got to load some supplies onto the shuttle."

She nodded. "I can certainly help with that."

There were only three floaters loaded with crates. Pushing and steering them by hand, they guided them from the starship's shuttle to his. Gina was very aware that he was watching her even as she was watching him.

He nodded. "It looks like you have some experience handling one of these." He used the thumb control on the handle to guide his through the shuttle door.

She chuckled. "I didn't have the cash to just pay for a passenger berth here. I took odd jobs to pay my way."

"Sorry about that. It was policy. We've had too many applicants who just wanted to see the Pit and could bamboozle the interviewer on Earth."

She nodded. "I get it. You wanted motivated people. It was fine. I'm not afraid to get my hands dirty."

Trane was relaxing a bit. This was still part of the interview process and he hadn't quite made up his mind about her.

When they finished loading and she stashed her travel bag. He asked, "Is that all your stuff?"

She nodded. "I chose items that packed tight. Better to do laundry than worry about lost bags out here where there aren't any stores."

"Well, you *can* order things from the catalog, but delivery time is... substantial."

"I can imagine."

Trane went to the piloting chair.

"You fly this yourself?"

"Everyone doubles up. Even if you're a specialist, you're expected to be able to do anything."

"Good, then let me watch." She sat next to him, watching as he worked.

He pointed to the desk-mounted display in front of him. "The Pit system is a nightmare to fly." A list of stations came up, with their masses.

He selected Pendulum station from the list and the computer gave a list of allowed targets and vectors.

Gina said, "I can see that there are no planets and you can't use the Pit as a target, but why can't you just put a tractor beam on Pendulum and be done with it?"

"The stations aren't all that massive and everything would be pulled out of their allotted orbits soon enough. Some of these pulls are to get us to our destination and some are to push other stations back into their proper orbits. The computer on Warehouse keeps track of it all. Most of us understand it, but the Nuren have their own TP procedures and really resent having to follow the Warehouse directives."

Gina nodded. "Sounds like you need another Warehouse-like mass in the system."

"You're not the first to suggest it, but there just aren't that many heavy lift starships that could get something like that here within our lifetimes. Warehouse was a lucky find, a rogue asteroid within slower-than-light range. Getting it into orbit was hard enough. The old-timers say there were a string of starships that popped into the system just long enough to be mass for the deceleration beams before leaping away again."

She chuckled. "Clever. And expensive."

Trane shrugged. "Everyone hopes for a fortune that will make it all worthwhile."

They shifted their beam target from one station to another.

She asked, "Has anyone made any discoveries yet?"

"Little stuff. The early stations swept up everything nearby—mainly pebbles and dust. It was a mix. Some were perfectly ordinary, others were … different. The labs here are still working on trying to make sense them."

She nodded. "How do you analyze alien elements with ordinary chemicals and diagnostics?"

"It's worse than that. None of them are pure samples of material from the other universe. By the time they've navigated through the wormhole, our physics has modified them. It's just a hybridized mix."

"I was wondering why I hadn't read any grand overview of the other physics."

"Maybe we'll get there. Maybe not."

"How often do new materials arrive?"

"Not often. The last one was big, a dust cloud puffed out of the throat and there was a mad dash by all the stations to try to collect as much of it as possible. The thinking was that if it turned out useful, it might have proved to be the most valuable substance in our universe." He chuckled. "Everyone was frantically throwing together scoops, magnetic or TP nets—everybody but Pendulum."

"Oh?"

"Yes, the boss ordered a high speed probe, a tiny little thing, to get there in the middle of the cloud, sweep up a sample and get it back to the lab as quickly as possible."

Trane had a slight smile. Gina asked, "So did Pendulum get what it needed?"

"Yes. As far as what we could tell, a lump of something like a rock went into the Pit on the other side and in the process of coming into our physics, decomposed into dust. Under our microscopes, it just looked like dust particles dissolving into even tinier dust particles. No explosion, no release of energy, they just... dissolved away."

"Is that normal?"

He chuckled, "Matter dwindling away leaving nothing but hard vacuum, no, not normal. But... this is other-universe stuff. Some of it explodes. The gas in the throat glows, probably as either interstellar hydrogen or something on the other side reacts to the change in physics. Everybody knows that if someone tries to take a Click leap engine apart that it'll explode. We still don't know the rules.

"That's what makes working at Pendulum so interesting. The boss owns the company outright and he's more interested in the physics than making a huge fortune off it. He probably has so much money already that this is just a hobby for him. We don't have to chase money. We chase the mystery."

"He's involved in the actual work?" she asked.

Trane nodded, and his grin slipped a little. "Yes, but not too intrusively. He lets us do our work, but he does visit the lab quite often."

Gina looked at him carefully. "You seem to have a reservation about that."

He didn't meet her eye, double-checking the navigation settings. "Um. I don't want to prejudice you before you've even met him."

"I can make my own decisions. What worries you?"

He glanced at her. "You're prettier than I was expecting. That might be a problem—but don't tell him I said that!"

"Oh? A womanizer?"

"Well… when Jason Kurt bought the half-completed Pendulum station from its original owners, he arrived with a companion and when she left a few months later, there was a chemist who caught his eye. She moved in with him for a while, but now she's gone too.

"When I read your resumé, and from what I've seen from you thus far I've been impressed, I'd really hate to lose you before you get your feet firmly planted here."

She waved her hand. "Believe me, I've got plenty of experience dodging the opportunists. I can look dowdy. I dressed up for my first impression here."

"Whatever you like. I need a physicist, not a model."

She nodded.

Jason Kurt. The computer records suggested Alpha had headed for the Pit when it was first discovered. Her research flagged a Luther Allen who had arrived back then and worked at the European Research Institute station. When he retired, he vanished off the passenger lists, but then this Jason Kurt arrived shortly after that with a suspiciously thin history. He was the same height and rough description as Allen, but came in as a rich executive on this entirely different station. This description as a womanizer cinched the case that he was Alpha, as far as she was concerned.

I'll need to get a good look at him before he notices me.

Dropping the Probe

Gina gasped, "Did they name Pendulum after the design of the station?"

On the display, it looked like a long metal rod with a circular weight on the end, just like the pendulum in a mechanical clock she'd seen on Earth in a museum.

"There's nothing official, but that's a common opinion. That's not a weight at the end. It's an empty space enclosed on all sides by sensors. We'll be bringing samples into the middle to be examined."

He docked on the other end, where there were access ports for three shuttles. There was a small one already using one of them.

Once they exited, Trane said, "Before you go to Employee Resources, come here and look at the Pit through a glass window. The computer displays always give the wrong impression."

He led her to a room just down the long central corridor.

She took in a breath. Not only was it a lot closer, but the color was different.

"Something looks … wrong."

He stared at it too. "I know. It's blue, but not like anything else in nature."

"What's it's temperature?"

"Cold. The color is deceptive. This is definitely not a star. The spectrum is very narrow, and totally not a black-body temperature. Galactic Lens has seen it from various distances and it's always the same—not cooling down or anything."

Gina shook her head. "I'm confused."

"Welcome to the club."

...

There were fifty-plus people at the station, every type from cooks to re-searchers and a medical doctor. She was grateful that the long-dead genetic researchers who built her made her blood so close to normal that nothing had ever shown up when she had been given physicals.

"Mr. Trane, I've moved in and they told me where to find you." She had changed to drab overalls and had her hair tied back in a bun.

He waved the ruler in his hand. "Just call me Douglas, or Doug. Come look at the design. This is a probe we're going to send into the Pit."

"People haven't done that yet?"

"Oh, there's been lots of probes. Even the discovery mission that first arrived at the Pit sent a capsule that swung by the throat on a tight elliptical orbit and tried to capture some of the gas."

He gave her a summary of what had been tried. Free-falling orbits that got close to the throat had worked, but nothing that entered the gas cloud had been all that successful. Any cameras or control systems failed, prob-ably because of the different physics.

"Plus there are the regulations to consider. Nobody is allowed to con-taminate the Pit's environment. So... no rockets. No outgassing of any kind. We've dropped probes into the Pit and when they get deep enough into the throat, we lose all contact. The Nurens sent a probe designed to fall through to the other side, then fall back to us, but even through the math looked good, it never returned."

She asked about the alternate physics.

"We can infer some of it by the size of the Pit itself. If this was a classi-cal Einstein-Rosen bridge with only twelve Earth-masses, then it would be tiny. Gravity itself has to be different on the other side, and the wormhole size is a compromise of some sort.

"It's frustrating that the gas itself blocks our view of the other side. If it was transparent, then we'd be able to look through with a good telescope and be able to find out all kinds of things."

"That's one of the things my probe is trying to accomplish."

They were building a purely mechanical probe with a variety of sensors. A shotgun approach hoping that at least something would return usable data.

The probe was going to be attached to a thousand-klom rope with a counter mass at the other end. Dropped with no orbital velocity straight down to the center, they'd use a tractor beam on the counter mass to slow it to a stop and pull it back, once it had entered the throat. The system rules prohibited any tractor beams from being aimed at the Pit itself, but short pulses of tractor could provide the limited-range pull that they needed.

"Of course, we have no idea how long the throat is. It might be light-years in length, for all we know. A thousand klom cable is the longest we can order from Vesta, but they're working on longer ones."

Douglas called it his probe, because he was the guy building it. But Jason Kurt had proposed the design.

...

Over the next couple of weeks, Gina was playing catch-up, helping Douglas and his team with the probe, but also reviewing every previous encounter with other-side matter.

Not being with her team half the time also gave her the opportunity to scout out the entire station and see what she could find out about Alpha. In a meeting room, there was a wall of photos, showing the construction of Pendulum station. It had arrived in sections, transported from a facility in orbit near Vesta, and then assembled here in the Pit system. Apparently, the original group who had started the project had gone bankrupt and Jason Kurt had bought them out and completed the assembly. She saw a couple of team photos with a younger Douglas Trane and two other people still on his team. In spite of the dozens of photos, there were none showing the owner.

One day, she overheard cook talking to her assistant. "Make sure the little shuttle is stocked. The boss is taking another joyride tomorrow."

"I'll need the code. He keeps that thing locked up."

It seemed that when Jason Kurt had arrived at Pendulum, he'd brought his own private shuttle with him. Nobody really knew what he did with it. But, with a little planning, she was able to be in a darkened room when he moved from his quarters to the docking port.

He was clearly distracted, carrying a small case, probably containing a computer or papers. It was her first opportunity to get a real look at his face. He was wearing makeup to appear older but if she hadn't the experience of doing the same, she might have missed it. The hair was tinted a little too.

That's Alpha, no doubt about it. If she'd met him somewhere with no warning, she might have been tempted to spend some time with him. He certainly had a fit body and no distracting irregular features. The body was fine. If he had a good personality, she had no doubt any woman would be intrigued.

She had to be ready. Doug said he came by the lab from time to time. Her own disguise needed to be perfect and she had to make sure she didn't betray her interest when he showed.

. . .

"You know how long it takes to get materials shipped in! When is the design going to be finished?" Frank Annes was the man who would bend the metal and polish the probe, once he was allowed to start. Thus far he'd spent all his time on the cable and counter weight.

Douglas shook his head. "I can't give you the final design because it hasn't been approved yet. We'll have a meeting tomorrow. Give the boss your concerns then."

He looked at Gina. "You'll need to be there too. The whole design team should be ready for any questions."

She nodded. Not only should she look the part, she needed to act like a new employee as well.

A few minutes later, she whispered to Evadean Stell, a metallurgist, "Dee, what's the dress code when the boss shows up? I'm new."

Dee brushed back her salt-and-pepper hair. "Hmm. Unless you're looking to get a promotion to be his 'personal assistant', I'd say your work clothes are fine. Look professional and neat, but there's no special attire."

The next day, they met in the conference room with the photos. Douglas spread out the design documents on the table. Jason Kurt was there before most people arrived. When the last man arrived, he tapped the table with his finger.

"Frank Annes, what's the status of the cable?"

Gina listened with interest. The cable and the counterweight had been manufactured in the Solar system. The counterweight had been a nickle-iron asteroid moved into L4 near Vesta and then melted in a solar furnace and then spun into a teardrop shape. The cable had five main strands, steel, carbon monofilament, and three different polymers. The idea was that if the otherside physics caused one or more of the strands to weaken, then the others would take up the slack.

As Douglas went over the design of the probe, the same philosophy was repeated. Many previous probes failed catastrophically when the otherside rules caused them to disintegrate. This one was slightly different in that they would be dipping it lightly into the throat of the Pit and then quickly hauling it back out.

There was no hull around the probe, just a sturdy framework with various sensors. Gina had worked on a clockwork camera that used a pinhole around a spinning cylinder. It wasn't so much designed to take a photo as it was to record a spiral track showing ambient light.

There were other mechanical sensors—all designed to return some kind of data even as they failed.

The boss never looked pleased. Finally, he said, "We need to double up on the sensors. I want timers on everything. I want to know when each kind of material fails."

Gina spoke, "Why?" Her camera, in particular was its own timer.

He turned to her. His eyes blinked, then he looked distracted, talking to the room. "Remnants from the other side retain some residue of their former laws of physics, even in our universe. We need to find out which of our materials will retain our physics, even in the alien environment. By putting timers on each experiment, maybe we'll be able to infer which of our materials last longest."

Douglas nodded. "So then in the next generation probe, we can build things out of the longest-lasting materials."

She could tell that even as Jason nodded agreement, he was hiding something.

After the boss had left, Douglas assigned the timers to Gina.

"You are closest to the clockwork stuff you used in the camera. Come up with as many different types of event timers as you can imagine."

The probe design was altered to leave attachment points for the timers and construction began. Gina knew she was suddenly on the high priority critical path before they could launch the probe.

She came up with as many designs as she could in short order and helped in the construction.

The whole purpose of the probe had changed. Instead of trying to see what was inside the throat of the Pit, the priority now was monitoring the change of physics in ordinary materials. The old sensors were still there, but she felt she had a license to make new ones.

One was like a harp, with strings of various materials, when a string decayed and broke, an attached pin would leave a mark on a rotating drum.

Another was a sealed fuse, burning in a tube that was woven throughout the probe, when something serious broke, it would snap the fuse either before or after it had burned. There were a dozen of these woven through the framework.

There was even a sand-filled hourglass laminated to a spinning plate. All kinds of timers—as many as she could get made before the deadline—were placed all over the probe.

On launch day, all the spinning elements were spun up with electric motors as the probe dropped toward the Pit and released when they reached the glowing cloud.

Everyone was watching as the probe grew hazy and vanished within the cloud. Jason Kurt was at the command of his little shuttle as he sent carefully timed tractor pulses to tug at the counterweight before it could vanish as well.

Gina had never flown a TP craft herself, although she knew the physics of it. She tensed up, fearing something would go wrong. The tractor pulse had to reach the weight and then be extinguished before it could reach the Pit itself.

Gradually, the weight and the rope began to pull out. No one knew how much tensile strength the rope had left, so he was being gentle with it.

It took several hours before the probe and the counterweight were spinning at a glacially slow rate near the Pendulum station. Gina noticed that several other shuttles were parked nearby. The different research stations watched each other, always hoping to see something useful.

Carefully, the Pendulum's dome opened up and the probe was pulled inside. It wasn't too surprising that the rope snapped during the process. The other shuttle was given the job of collecting the rope and counterweight. They would be examined carefully as well.

Douglas pointed. "Would you look at that!" The probe was twisted, as if some massive force had caught it up in a whirlpool.

Dispute

"The rope still had significant tensile strength, but only from the carbon and iron cables. The main problem is that they were brittle. No bending allowed. By the time we wound the cable back onto that monstrous spool, the Pit end of it had broken fifty times." Douglas shook his head. "Disposal is going to be a problem."

Jason shook his head. "We can sell it as 'Pit treated steel' or something. There are plenty of research teams who will bid on our cast-offs. It takes a serious commitment to set up a facility here and most can't afford it."

He then pointed to Gina. "How did your timers work out?"

"Surprisingly well." She was ready with charts and photos. Her camera gave her a view showing the foggy background with the framework of the probe itself in the foreground. The raw recordings on the cylinder had to be run through the computer to generate human-usable images, but with some interpolation, it could even produce a compressed video of the scene.

"Notice how the probe's structure began to twist right about at the time the cable started to pull it back out. The deceleration and the twist are somehow related."

Her timers gave lots of data, before they failed. It would take a long time to decode what the data told them.

"Anything that used spring-wound mechanisms failed quickly. The fuses failed in several places, but not when they were in direct contact with a large structural beam. It's was obvious, but the more mass clumped together, the more resistant to otherside forces. More dense metals seem more resistant to the decay."

Jason nodded. "That's what I was hoping for."

"We can't count on that. There are still many puzzling variations."

...

There were several weeks where nothing was done other than analyze which materials were best for resisting the corrosive effects of otherside physics. The boss was there much more frequently than he had been before.

Gina shook her head. "No, the carbon monofilament tensile strength shows that there's more than just mass involved."

Jason frowned. "But your figures show a strong correlation between mass and delayed decay. We can just go with that for the next probe. Order more tungsten and osmium to shield the more sensitive instruments."

"Yes, we can do that, but we'll end up with a probe so heavy that the cable can't pull it back out without breaking."

He sniffed. "If we could get a tractor beam deeper into the throat, then we wouldn't have that problem."

She waved her hand. "That's a political issue. Take it up with the Warehouse manager. I'm just saying that with the rules we have, that we need to understand the real reason the carbon-to-carbon bonds resist the otherside influence as well as they do.

"Personally, I'd be worried about sending a tractor beam deep into the Pit. TP crystals came from the Pit originally, didn't they? There could be catastrophic interactions that we haven't a way to predict."

"If the Nuren were in charge, we wouldn't have these restrictions."

After the long, contentious meeting finished up, as Gina was collecting her materials, she heard Jason sigh. It was slight, but she noticed it.

She didn't meet his eyes, but she said, "Why do you look at me that way?"

"Sorry. It's just that you remind me of someone."

"Who?"

"It doesn't matter. A relationship that didn't work out. Someone who argued like you do."

There was no one else around, but she didn't want to push it right then. An ordinary employee wouldn't get too nosy about her boss's personal history. She gathered her things and left the room.

...

Douglas was excitedly making plans for the next probe—stronger and heavier than the last one. The structural framework was designed to bend smoothly if it were twisted like the last one. They were ordering 3000 kloms of a new cable—this one with carbon, steel, and nickel as the primary strands.

Jason was showing up frequently, chatting with Douglas and the other team members. As he finished up, he waved at Gina. "I need to talk about your camera."

They went to one of the little side rooms and sat at the table. He asked, "Can you double or triple the resolution of your camera? I'd like to maybe record on multiple tracks as well, using different light-sensitive chemicals. The last time, the contrast was clearly taking a hit as we got deeper into the Pit, and I'd like to at least be able to see if there are any other objects in the throat."

She nodded. "I've been considering other chemicals already. Do I get a bigger attachment space?"

Jason frowned. "I'd rather not. Smaller is better."

She sighed. "We're making a bigger probe, but with smaller instruments. The weight difference for a bigger camera would be trivial compared with the beefed up framework."

"I'm just planning ahead. When we can reliably get instruments back, we'll try larger cargo."

"What? Materials that get shifted? Have you found a market for Pit-treated materials?"

He shrugged. "No, it's just that in the best of all worlds, we could make a protected environment large enough to carry a passenger."

Gina shook her head. "That's crazy. We're too far away from being able to do that."

"I'm patient."

She shook her head firmly. "That's suicide."

"Why? We live in outer space, in a vacuum where our blood would boil without protection. Why can't we imagine visiting a place where physics is different?"

"Because we can't just shield away a different reality! Life as we know it can't exist on the other side. We've proven that with our own experiments. Just a few kloms into the throat and chemistry doesn't work the same. Life—" she thumped her chest, "—can't exist there."

"But your timers show that it could last a little while, when surrounded by enough of the right kind of material. Long enough for me to see the other side."

"*You* see? You're planning to do this yourself?"

He shrugged. "Somebody's got to be first. Why not me?"

She shook her head. She had wondered what it was that had attracted Alpha to the Pit. "So it's just pride, then?"

He hesitated. "A little. What's wrong with wanting to leave a mark on the universe?"

She looked at him carefully. "That sounds like someone thinking about dying." This was Alpha. What could he be thinking? He was the ultimate survivor. There was no way he'd dive into a fatal environment—unless she'd totally misread him.

"Everyone thinks about death, at one time or another."

"Not you." She put down her notepad. "I'm not working on some megalomaniac's suicide project. I quit."

She walked out.

Douglas saw her stalking out into the corridor and hurried to chase her down.

"Gina! What's wrong? Did he try something… inappropriate?"

She shook her head. "No. Don't ask. I'm just not sure that this is the right project for me. I should never have come here."

He was walking beside her, trying to keep pace. "You're perfect for this. I don't want to lose you."

She waved him off. "I'm done for the day. Maybe done entirely."

...

Gina seethed as she packed. It would be a few days until the regular shuttle arrived from the warehouse and she'd have to do some serious juggling to get transport back to Luna.

I really blew my stack there. I messed up.

Maybe it was because she had misjudged him. Since she was made aware of the existence of Alpha, she'd been building a model of him in her mind— some genius, amoral, larger-than-life guy who was somehow related to her.

I was buying into his vision—that he and I were somehow destined to be together. I was expecting more of him.

But he was smaller than she'd expected. Yes, he was a genius, but this idea of making a mark on humanity with a grand gesture—something that would kill him—that was just a failure's way out.

Maybe she should have seen it earlier. His body was forever young, but maybe he was tired and mentally fatigued. She'd seen his lapses. In his prime, she would never have been able to track him down. He was taking shortcuts when he dropped one identity and took up another. He had favorite names that he repeated from time to time.

She stuffed another outfit into her bag and closed her eyes.

It was hard packing to leave. She'd swapped identities many times, but those times, she was just walking away. This time she'd have to say her goodbyes and make her excuses for leaving. It was harder.

There was a knock on the door. Mary came in, fire in her eyes.

"What did he do? I've put up with him for years now, but driving you off is the limit!"

Gina shook her head. "It isn't what you think. It was nothing… personal. I just found out we have very different philosophies about this project and I don't want to be part of it anymore."

Mary stared at her. "There has to be more to this. He did something. I'm sure of it."

Gina hugged her, fighting the edge of tears. "I'm sorry. I just had an argument with Mr. Kurt about the way the project was going. Seriously, it was just about the probe. He's the boss, the owner. He wins, so I've got to leave."

Mary crossed her arms. "Well, I've had plenty of disputes about the way things work, but he's never fired me for it."

"He didn't fire me. I quit." And that was all she was willing to say about it.

Mary was just the first to come by and check on her. Gina appreciated the feeling of having people concerned for her, but there was so much she couldn't share. It was difficult to keep her story straight when she was hiding so much.

She ducked out and went to the room with the big windows to get a little privacy. She sat in the dark and looked out. The Pit was hanging there, not even bright enough to block out the stars. It was such a mystery and she hated that she couldn't stay and be part of the effort to probe its interior. She just couldn't allow herself to be sucked into his scheme. She was like those earlier Pit probes—she just wanted to swing by and sample, rather than be sucked into the unknown.

Maybe it had all been a mistake to come here. What happened to her idea of confronting him for all his past sins?

He's not a wayward child. He's a lot older than I am. I'm not going to change him.

For the first time in decades, she felt like a teenager again, uncertain about the future and fearful that she was the only one who didn't have their act together. By the calendar, she was older than most of them, but they still looked at her as an inexperienced young woman.

But with Jason Kurt, she *knew* he had the edge on her.

"Gina?" The door edged open. It was him.

"What do you want?" she asked.

"I don't want Douglas Trane and the rest of the crew to mutiny. I want to talk with you some more."

She stared out at the Pit. "Is there anything more to say?"

"Yes, quite a bit. But there really isn't any privacy on the station. Could I talk you into coming aboard my shuttle where secrets can't be overheard? If I still can't convince you to stay, then I'll take you to Warehouse myself and you won't have to wait for the regular shuttle."

She wondered about what secrets he was talking about. Had he deduced her real identity? If so, then yes, they needed a private place to talk.

She sighed. "Okay."

Secret Scoop

Jason Kurt's private yacht was smaller than the cargo shuttle, but it was all living space. It was bigger than any of the living quarters in the station. Rumor had suggested that he had brought the shuttle with him when he arrived and she could certainly believe it. She was surprised that he didn't just stay on board rather than in his official quarters.

On a display shelf there were several items from the Pit, including the twisted hourglass timer that she'd designed. It was fascinating how it had been bent into an entirely different shape.

She reached out for it.

"Don't touch that. There's still enough otherness leaking out of it that I lost some skin on my fingertips when I tried it."

She nodded, letting her hand drop. He gestured toward a seat. They sat facing each other.

He grimaced. "Is it the project you're disillusioned with, or is it just me?"

She sighed. She had to be blunt. "It's you. The project is fascinating. I just can't support someone headed toward death."

He frowned. "I think I must have explained things badly. I'm not trying to commit suicide. I really want to find a way to shield the effects so that we can safely visit the other side and return."

She shrugged, unconvinced. "Even when there's shielding, every atom begins to change." She gestured toward the timer on the shelf. "Shielding may slow down the decay, but damage starts immediately. When we're talking biological systems, we can't afford any decay."

He asked, "What will you do when you leave here?"

"I'll probably go help my grandfather with his project."

"What's that?"

"Medical research. It's life-and-death to some people. I'd be on the side of life."

He considered a bit, then said, "Can you keep a secret?"

"Easily. It's second nature to me."

He nodded.

He opened up a computer display. "This is a Nuren report they sent back to their home world. I managed to intercept and decode it."

She nodded, not really surprised by the spying. All the research stations monitored each other. That he'd decoded it wasn't surprising either. Human encryption was orders of magnitude better than what most Galactics used. Only the races that had purchased human computer systems were starting to use the better versions.

As she read the report, struggling with the translated grammar, she could tell that the Nuren had used secret TP density waves, in violation of the Pit administrative rules, to map the interior of the Pit's throat. Mass and gravity were one of the few things common to both universes, although the intensities were vastly different. Probably Jason had no interest in alerting the warehouse about this violation of the rules. He'd probably have done the same if he could have gotten away with it. Let the Nuren take the penalty. He'd take the data.

The map showed that there was something more dense barely orbiting inside, near the center of the throat.

Jason said, "Sometime in the past, some object or objects were stranded in the throat and gas friction gradually caused that mass to come to rest at the center.

"I'm ordering Douglas to modify the second probe to allow for it to collect part of this denser mass and allow us to retrieve it. We're the research station likely to get there first."

She asked, "Which side did it come from?"

He nodded. "That's a good question. A random object, like an asteroid, falling from outside the Pit system should probably have enough inertia to speed on through, but I suppose there could be something slow-going that might be trapped by gas friction.

"Or then again, it could be artificial.

"I could easily imagine losing our probe to an accident, and it could oscillate for a while in the gas. We know the Pit has been discovered previously in ancient times. The Humans were just the first to go public with it and make the Galactic claim. This could be the residue from researchers like us. It could also be from the other side."

Everything from random rocks and asteroid masses to radioactive particles traveled through the Pit at random, and that's what the relics from the other side looked like as well.

She giggled. "Maybe it's a lost probe from the other side."

"If there is life in the other universe, and if it ever developed space travel."

"Gina, I really need your help. Make me a camera that will show this object, even if the probe fails to retrieve a sample."

She sighed, staring at the crude map of the high density area. It was in range of their next probe. The challenge had her fired up.

"Okay, you got me. I want to stay—but only if there's never any hint of any suicide missions!"

...

Jason went back to his shuttle after walking Gina back to her quarters and notifying Douglas that she had changed her mind about leaving. He'd been exaggerating about the team threatening to mutiny, but they'd been very upset.

This girl was different from the others. She was more mature than she looked and was immune to his good looks and wealth.

But what nagged at him was the way she appeared to know him. When he'd mentioned thoughts of mortality, she said, "But not you." *She's convinced I am on the side of death and destruction, although there is nothing in Jason Kurt's history to suggest that.*

Her moral compass aligning with life vs. death wasn't unusual, but he rarely had someone throw it into his face. *By that philosophy, I'm a very bad man indeed.*

Maybe it was just her superficial resemblance to Billie that threw him off. There were probably an endless number of girls who resembled her, but that didn't mean anything. It was impossible a new Beta had appeared unexpectedly. *If this is an adult Billie, her makeup is flawless.*

Once back on the shuttle, he put away the Nuren report and made sure nothing was out of place. Then he asked his computer to run a second-level background check on Gina Parker.

...

The design of the probe came together quickly, once Jason held a top-secret meeting with Gina, Douglas and a couple of others where directly involved with structural design.

Jason told them, "This capture-and-return mission has to be kept totally under wraps. Nobody else, other than the Nuren, know about the mass caught in the throat. If it gets out, there will be a flood of poorly designed probes in a rush to grab the first sample. Warehouse might even put a moratorium on probes until they think about if for a few years."

Everyone was on board. Douglas quickly came up with a self-actuating scoop that needed no power or control to operate, just direct contact with a resisting medium. As long as the hinge didn't seize up, it should work.

The new cable was scheduled to arrive in a couple of weeks, so that was their deadline for getting everything else ready. Some of the original sensors were put on hold. Gina's camera went on high priority.

Jason was very aware that all the team members were watching him closely, so he kept his interactions with Gina very simple and professional.

The probe was quickly coming together, hovering in the weightless center of the sensor bay. They had all the hatches sealed and the place pressurized so that people could work on the mechanism and sensors without having to suit up for vacuum.

Gina floated next to her camera, aligning it so that the scooping operation would be centered in its view. She looked at the array of cameras pointed at the probe.

"Doug?"

"Yes?" He was floating near the scoop, manually working the cups, verifying that the scoop would close and lock on their sample with just a simple push.

"Are we planning on pulling the probe back in here after we pull it back?"

He looked around. "Hmm. An unknown quantity of unknown material that has been known to explode in the past. Maybe we should set up an outside examination area, at least at first."

The sensor bay was opened up and workers in suits dismounted a third of the bay's cameras and moved them to a simple open grid floating a few hundred meters away from the station.

And then the day came. The Warehouse shuttle arrived, steering the huge spool of cable with short TP bursts. Douglas and Frank handled the task of hooking up the counterweight and the probe. Jason used his shuttle to push the probe, slowing down its orbital velocity to zero as the cable unspooled behind it.

As before, other organizations had shuttles in the vicinity, watching the progress. There was considerable interest since it hadn't been all that long since the earlier probe. Just a month earlier, the European Research Institute had sent an orbiting probe around the Pit, broadcasting radio and beaming laser beams through the top layers of the atmosphere. All stations had done their best to record what they could receive and the data was pooled for common use. Jason was partly afraid that the dense mass in the center would be detected that way, but nobody had reported it.

This time, Jason followed the counterweight half-way to the Pit, careful to guide and slow the fall of the probe. None of the other shuttles knew what he was up to, but he wanted his probe to come to a complete stop just as it reached the calculated location of the target.

It was practically imperceptible, but when contact occurred, the tension in the cable changed and he was able to notice it in his tractor beams when that quiver traversed the cable as a sound wave.

He slowly began pulling the counterweight, using the Pendulum station as the back-beam mass. One mistake and the cable would snap and he'd lose the probe.

"Coming back out." He was sure Gina was waiting for that acknowledgment. She never fully trusted him. She had overreacted, thinking he would commit suicide.

By the time he caught up with the station, he was still moving relatively fast, he had to slow the whole cable length to match the stations orbit. He carefully adjusted the probe so that it would come to relative rest near the external examination area. As it stopped, matching the station's orbit, he was still 3,000 kloms away and he needed to make his way back without any of his beams disturbing the cable.

He monitored radio communication as his team was exiting the airlock in their spacesuits to go detach the cable and take their initial look at the sample they'd hopefully captured.

He was also monitoring any conversations that might spill from the other shuttles. The humans would be using normal encrypted messaging, but the Nuren might let something slip. They might be very aware that his probe had touched the exact place that they had detected some unknown mass. How would they react to that?

Douglas was reporting that this time, the cable hadn't snapped, but they still were going to be very careful about letting it bend. He had detached the probe and connected the cable to the spool. Gathering it all back up would take days. Jason sent out a general broadcast alerting everyone in the Pit system that the cable and counterweight system would be slowly pinwheeling in its orbit near the Pendulum station. Probably all the pilots were aware of the hazard, but it didn't hurt to send the warning.

The radio chatter confirmed that once again the probe had been twisted, although the new one had held up better than the other one.

Using the mass of the Warehouse and two other stations as anchor points for his beams, Jason brought his shuttle back on a return path to Pendulum.

The crew was taking detailed photos of the probe and especially its sample and he wished he could see a video of it, but that hadn't been a priority.

Gina's voice said, "I'm going in to detach my camera from its mount. The sample appears stable."

Douglas said, "Be careful. Try not to jostle anything. I'm on the other side."

"Got it."

Jason eased his shuttle closer and with his cameras, he could see several suited figures moving closer to the probe.

And then the image flashed. The camera went dead. His shuttle's computer said, "Radiation warning!"

Afterburn

"Gina!"

There was no response. He switched cameras and was able to see that the station and the probe were still there. Something had happened, but it hadn't destroyed everything.

"External crew, report!" That was from Wilson on the Pendulum station on the radio. There was no response.

Jason went to the controls and tapped lightly with the beams bringing his shuttle up close. He grabbed his emergency gear, basically sealed overalls and a helmet with five minute's worth of air and opened the airlock.

His joints stiffened up from the internal pressure, but he could still maneuver. He grabbed his gripper and opened the airlock.

Using the gripper, a hand-held TP maneuvering gadget, he pulled himself to the probe. He could see two things. The scoop part of the probe had been ripped apart, and Gina in her spacesuit, curled up around her camera.

"Gina!" he called, but she didn't react.

He pulled her close, and her arms waved in reaction. When her faceplate turned toward his, her mouth moved, but there was nothing over the radio.

He grabbed her arm and began towing her back to the shuttle. She didn't let go of her grip on the camera. She tugged with her free hand and made helmet-to-helmet contact.

Faintly, she said, "Radio is out. Maybe radiation."

He nodded.

She pulled hard again, "I'll heal quickly, you know why. No doctor."

He nodded. It was all the confirmation he needed. Somehow, impossibly, Gina was another Beta.

I can't lose her!

He fished her into the airlock, almost ready to get her immediately to the station, and then another thought intruded. *The rest of the exterior team are out there. Gina will hate me if I leave them behind.*

He just pointed at the airlock controls and went back outside. Probably she could get herself into the pressurized cabin and he didn't have much air left in his emergency helmet.

As he raced to find Douglas, he called to Wilson, "I've recovered Gina, alive. I'm going for Trane. Give me a list of everyone else outside."

Douglas was drifting in the hunched over, weightless, sleeping position. By the time he'd dragged the unresponsive man back to the shuttle, his own air supply alarm was blaring in his ear. Gina had cycled the airlock for him, so there was no delay getting them both inside.

As the pressure came up. Wilson called, "Mary and Frank were both outside, but we've recovered them, both alive. How is Douglas?"

"Unresponsive. I won't know until I get him into the cabin. I'll be docked shortly. Send a floater to carry him to sick bay. Gina is ambulatory."

Jason ripped off his emergency gear as soon as he could and began to unfasten Trane's helmet.

Gina was at the inner airlock door. "How is he?"

"He's breathing, unconscious."

Gina tried to help move him inside, but Jason could see her unsteadiness.

"No! Don't help. Go stretch out on the bed. We'll be unloading him just as soon as I dock. You should go to the sick bay as well."

She shook her head. "No. They might find something."

He sighed. He knew her concerns all too well. "Just rest then. I'll be back just as soon as I can. I'll make up some kind of excuse."

Less than a minute later, they docked and Jason hoisted Douglas, still in his suit, out the airlock.

Wilson was there with the floater and a couple of workers. They raced him down to the sick bay.

Wilson asked, "Where's Gina?"

Jason growled. "She's being stubborn. I'll try to get her to get checked out as soon as possible. But now, I'm worried about Douglas."

The sick bay was crowded. The doctor checked Douglas's vitals. "It's looking like a radiation flash. Larry and Mary are getting standard treatment, but I don't know how bad Douglas is."

Jason nodded. "Be prepared to give him a transfusion. Red blood cells are vulnerable."

The doctor frowned. "Do you have medical training? If not, leave me alone to do my job."

Jason nodded and backed out. It was a good excuse to get back to Gina.

...

His message alerts were flashing on the display, but he ignored them to check on her. She was asleep and he worked cautiously, checking her temperature and taking a blood sample. Respiration and heart seemed slightly elevated, but that's what he expected.

The messages were frantic. The radiation burst had been detected all over the Pit system. He sent out a summary, acknowledging that they had scooped up some higher density material from inside the Pit and that it had exploded some time after they had brought it back to the station. He emphasized their safety precautions but told them of the radiation exposure for the external team.

Warehouse declared a temporary moratorium on Pit probes. Pendulum was ordered to supply an incident report with full details.

Jason was having a hard time worrying about the paperwork. Another Beta had arrived. Three times before, he'd been filled with hope only to have her die, devastating him. He could sense the Old Man hovering in the back of his mind, just waiting to swap him out with another persona if he couldn't keep things together.

I can't lose Gina. I can't.

She stirred and mumbled, "Did we get the data?"

He moved over and sat on the edge of the bed, checking her temperature. She was slightly warmer on her right side.

"Your camera is right over there. Unless the radiation wiped it, the data should still be good. Everyone is more concerned about you and the others right now."

"Doug?"

"And Mary and Larry. You all have bad radiation exposure. Douglas is the worst. I'm sure we'll need to give him a transfusion."

Gina nodded, looking like she was suffering through a headache. "I should donate—"

"No, you got a normally fatal dose. You're not to get out of that bed. I'll be your doctor for now."

"I'm immune."

"No! Have you had radiation exposure before?"

She shook her head.

"Then believe me, you're not immune. You have cell damage. It's just that people like us recover more quickly. How old are you?"

She grimaced. "Not supposed to ask a lady that."

"This century?"

She nodded.

"Then just take the advice of someone with more experience. You need rest. Expect bland meals, fluid drips, and bad-tasting medicines for now."

"I need to decode my camera."

"So I'll be your lab assistant, but you need rest. I'll get you a computer you can use in bed."

"But the camera—"

"I'll take the camera to get it fed into the system. You rest!"

...

Jason was happy to see her sleep, but she was tossing fitfully and reacting to every noise he made. He winced as there was a knock on the outer airlock door.

He cleared his throat. "I'd better answer that."

Outside in the port access tunnel were two men, Josh Osso with a floater containing food supplies from the galley, and Dr. Lee.

Jason said, "Can you be quiet? Gina needs her rest."

The doctor said, "That's why I came. She was close to the explosion. Surely she has radiation exposure and she hasn't come by to be checked out."

"Earlier you asked if I had medical training. Yes, I have. I knew your clinic already had too much to handle with the other three crew and I had already done a quick check on Gina."

He glanced at one face and then the other. "I need you to keep quiet about this, but she shows signs that she was exposed on the right side of her body. There is some inflammation and her skin is reacting to it as well."

"Then I need to see her immediately."

Jason held up his hand. "I don't know if you're aware, but this shuttle was fitted out as a rich man's yacht. That's why I brought it with me to the Pit system. I can live on it indefinitely and it has an excellent medical tool kit. Both she and I are confident that I can handle her treatment here without overburdening your clinic's facilities."

Josh nodded slightly. He was one of the very few who had seen the inside.

Jason continued, "In addition, Gina is a bit self-conscious about her appearance and would rather stay out of sight until she heals a bit."

Dr. Lee frowned. "Still, I really need to see her."

Jason nodded. "I understand." He raised his voice. "Gina! Dr. Lee is coming in. Josh, you can go ahead and stock the pantry as well."

They entered.

Gina had pulled the sheet over her head, only her arms were exposed.

The doctor came closer and in his calm bedside voice, he requested permission to check her condition.

Gina's voice was a little weak, but she was holding it together. "Okay, but… wait until Josh is done, okay?"

"May I check your pulse, then?"

He checked pulse and temperature on her exposed arms as Josh hurried to finish. When he backed his hover out, Gina tugged the sheet off her face.

"Sorry, I'm afraid a got a little sunburn out of this."

Her face was definitely redder on the right side.

Jason said, "I've already done a blood test, and I've given her a unit of Oxy as a precaution."

The doctor looked over Jason's records and nodded. "Can I check your med cabinet?"

After a few more questions, the doctor was content to leave her under Jason's care. In some ways the shuttle's medical supplies were better than his, and he was already overwhelmed by the three other patients.

When he left and Jason resealed the airlock, Gina whispered, "You didn't give me much warning. I'm vain about my appearance?"

He shrugged. "I was sure you could hear me. Is your facial flush natural?"

She shook her head. "I pinched a few veins and forced my heart to speed up a bit." She put her hand on her forehead. "Gave me a headache."

Jason said, "I'll try to keep everyone out until you officially heal."

"I'd rather have an excuse to check on Doug and the others."

"I'll see what I can do, but I'll go check on him myself here in a few minutes." He took her wrist and checked her pulse himself.

She looked at him with a narrow gaze. "I expect details."

He nodded.

...

Douglas opened his eyes to Jason staring at him.

He coughed, and whispered, "If I don't make it, shoot me through to the other side."

Jason chuckled. "Well, you do look like death itself, but that's mainly because your blood has been replaced with Oxy. It's a shame they can't make artificial blood with the right shade of red to it. But you're more valuable here on this side. Besides, we don't want the otherside aliens to think we all look like you, do you?"

Douglas tried to smile. "I guess not." He took a few breaths. "Gina? The others?"

"She got a dose herself, but she's recuperating. Larry and Mary are in much better shape that you. They were further away when it happened. Dr. Lee is checking everyone in the station, but only you four were really close enough to get the effects."

"What happened?"

Jason shrugged. "Gina will be working on her camera. We recorded other video from the moment the probe arrived until when it blew up. We lost a few cameras. I'll be reviewing those shortly. Warehouse is demanding answers, so I'll have to come up with them soon."

Douglas closed his eyes.

Jason said, "Don't worry, you'll get the best possible care. Just rest."

There had been many times in the past when he'd lost workers and not worried a minute about it. This time was different, not because of Doug or the others, but because Gina would blame him if they died. She was that kind of person, he was sure.

He checked on the rest of them and confirmed that none of the crew on the station at the time showed any radiation effects.

Dr. Lee said, "I should check you as well."

Jason shook his head. "I was too far away and my shuttle is well shielded."

Recovery

Jason sat on the edge of the bed and pointed to the screen. "We got over a minute of good video between the time that the probe was moved into the range of the external cameras and when it exploded."

Gina was propped up on her pillows, staring intently at the image. "Doesn't look like much. Sort of a gray mass."

"Switch to thermal."

She tapped the key. "I see, there's a hotspot, and it's growing."

When the explosion wiped the image, she backed up the video and zoomed in as close as possible in visual light. "Just a black blemish, at first."

Jason nodded, "But it's growing. Just part of the sample was unstable."

She sighed. "Do you have scissors and a razor?"

"Yes, why?"

"That camera caught more than just the sample in the scoop. It showed me dismounting my camera. I ought to have gotten a much worse exposure than Doug did. I need to lose my hair."

"It was a fatal exposure, for a normal human."

. . .

Carlos Leñera of Warehouse Management, formerly a planetologist with Galactic Lens, was seated across from Jason at the conference table.

Carlos asked, "How did you know that there was a substance inside the throat?"

Jason shrugged. "Well, as you know, we not only analyze the data from our own probes, but also any other data that we might come across."

"None of the other stations had reported seeing anything other than the gas cloud."

Jason smiled. "Perhaps none had *reported* anything."

Carlos sighed. "I miss the days of academic open exchange of information."

"Academics can't afford a research station in the Pit system."

"You analyzed the radio signals from the European orbiter, didn't you?"

"I can't really say at this time."

Carlos tapped the table. "If we'd known, we would have insisted on better safety precautions."

"We took extra precautions. Our ordinary methodology was to bring a sample into our sensor dome. We set up this external station just for this very reason."

There was a knock on the door and it opened before Jason could respond.

Gina appeared, in a plain, full-length gown with arms covered. Her head was wrapped with gauze only revealing her eyes, mouth and the red hair on the left side.

"Gina! What are you doing out of bed?"

She seated herself next to Jason. "I'm the camera designer. If you're going to show the images, then I'm the one who should be doing the presentation!"

Carlos chuckled. "That sounds like a researcher."

Jason wagged his finger. "Okay, but just that, and then back to bed. I'll call someone to help you get back."

"I'll get started then."

She tapped her computer keys and the design of the camera displayed on the wall. She explained the rotating drum sensor with its five tracks of different chemicals to provide redundancy in case the otherside influences caused the chemicals to fail to react.

"It's lucky that I did that, because the radiation blast wiped out three of them and degraded the others. The resulting video has poor resolution."

And then she showed the approach video as the probe approached the denser mass in the throat of the Pit. Colors shifted and faded due to the drum's rotation, but the image was solid.

Carlos gasped, "That's a manufactured object!"

"Yes," she said. "It appears to be a metal object a hundred times larger than our probe, but its mass is much less than that. It's like a marshmallow, only somewhat more dense than water. Watch as the scoop activates."

The mechanical scoop cut into the surface easily and almost instantly, the probe began backing out.

There was an obvious divot left in the surface.

"It's been damaged," Carlos griped.

Jason said, "Just slightly, and I'm glad we didn't haul the whole thing back out. No telling how big that blast would have been then. Something in that sample explodes in our normal space."

Carlos thought a moment and then said, "This is too big to hide. There has to be life in the other universe. This is proof."

Jason nodded. "You'd better be prepared for dozens of organizations and other Galactic races wanting to dip their own probes in, wanting to get a piece of it."

Gina stayed a few more minutes to answer questions about her camera and then Jason called for Josh Osso to take her back to the shuttle.

Carlos asked, "How much radiation did she take?"

Jason said, "She's losing her hair and has skin burns, but she's recovering nicely. It's Douglas Trane that I'm worried about. He got a much more intense blast and he needs better treatment than what we can provide here."

"We can take him to the Warehouse clinic."

Jason shook his head. "I've already scheduled his return to Earth. When Starship Lisbon arrives in two days, he'll be on it and taken to Berlin Central Hospital a day later. I've made arrangements for a direct return. That's the best place in the Solar system for radiation treatment."

...

"Have you apologized to Douglas and the others?" Gina asked, once they were alone in the shuttle and he mentioned sending him back to Earth for hospitalization.

He hesitated. "Perhaps not."

"Why not? Because they're human? Are you just getting Douglas out of your hair so you won't have to watch him die on the station?"

He winced. "No, that's not it. I don't apologize because I'm just not used to it."

She nodded. "You move freely among humans, but you don't live with them. And don't talk about your girlfriends! You know they give up on you fast enough."

He frowned, almost said something, and then walked over to his computer when it beeped, and tapped on the keys.

"Gina Parker's background holds up."

"Thank you. Did you only check it recently?"

"Oh, I started some time back, but the data just arrived. The records show one thing, but your DNA shows something else."

"You checked the DNA yourself? You know that's illegal, don't you?"

He sniffed. "I had to know for sure."

"And I could hardly complain about it, but Grandfather would be very disappointed in you."

He frowned. "Who is this 'Grandfather'?"

She shook her head. "You don't get to ask that yet. I'm not finished testing you."

He looked intrigued. "You're testing me?"

"Yes. Your history is … disconcerting. But I had to check you out myself. The records might have gotten things wrong."

"I've taken great care to leave no history behind."

"And my big question is why? Do you want to hide the horrible things you've done in the past? Or do you want to be free to do even more horrible things in the future?"

...

Gina walked beside the floater as they transferred Douglas to the shuttle taking him to the starship.

He took her hand. "You ought to come with Mary and me. You obviously got a bad dosage."

"I'll be fine. I think the explosion must have been asymmetrical or something because I'm already healing. I can't have gotten as much of the blast as you did."

He sighed. "I just worry that I'll never come back."

Jason said, "I'm sorry, Douglas. I should have insisted on more safety precautions. Warehouse is really beating me up about that.

"And don't worry about coming back here. Your treatment and return transport is already paid for, if you want to use it. The job will be waiting if you still want it. But you might be too famous.

"Proof that there are aliens in the other universe is just hitting the news and you and Mary will be the only ones they can interview. It was your probe that made the discovery after all."

Douglas gave a sour smile. "Thanks a lot."

...

After the Warehouse shuttle left, Gina sat down on a bench.

"Are you tired?"

She nodded. "I can fake it, but I've never felt so underpowered before."

"You're pushing your limits. You need more sleep."

She shook her head. "I want to see the probe up close. Can you take me there?"

Jason frowned. "I've got a team scheduled to go examine it for residual radiation tomorrow, now that we've got the Warehouse snoops out of our hair."

"Your shuttle has adequate radiation sensors. I just have a feeling we're missing something."

He shrugged. "You're probably right, but I don't want to slow down your recovery."

Still, they went inside the shuttle and Jason alerted his people that they were going to do a brief fly-by of the probe.

Once he turned off the radio, he said, "Now we're disconnected. I know you've been wanting to talk about something. Nobody can overhear us."

The shuttle pushed off gently. There was no need for speed.

"You can ask me anything."

Gina reclined in her seat. She looked at the ceiling. "Tell me about the good things you've done."

He sniffed. "You don't think I have any examples? I've lived a long time."

Checking the approach to the probe, he considered and then said, "There was the time Sally Velume fell into a pit when we were exploring a cave in Africa." He followed that tale with another where a different companion came down with appendicitis while on a hike and he had to carry her out of the forest on his back.

Gina raised her hand. "Keep thinking of examples, but I need to look at the probe right now."

Under a zoomed image, she found many gray deposits where the other-side residue had been caught on the framework of the probe. "The explosion was not that energetic. It didn't vaporize any of the probe and it just threw the residue in all directions."

Jason got on the radio and sent word to the Pendulum workers. "Prepare workers to scrape up our sample and get it into the lab as soon as possible."

He smiled to Gina. "That ought to keep a dozen researchers happy."

She nodded. "Make sure they look for any discolored spots. We don't want a repeat of the radiation flare."

While they waited, Jason told the tale of the balecat and the school teacher he'd saved from the ignorant farmers.

Gina shook her head. "It sounds like most of the people you've rescued have been lovers or just people you need for some reason or another."

"Well, you know about the merfolk, back on Earth, don't you. They would have gone extinct except for me."

He described how he had given the artificial people pride and a sense of identity with faked RNA racial memory and a few dummy artifacts he'd planted in the ocean for them to discover.

Gina knew a little about the merpeople. Everything she knew were reports about how angry and defensive they were about how land people perceived them. They weren't very popular. As humanity was expanding rapidly and looking outward toward the stars, the merpeople were stuck in the idea of defending their position in the sea. They hadn't even tried to migrate to the seas of Luna and Mars, even though they could handle the environment.

She said, "And it sounds like you only helped them because they were artificial, like us. Have you ever tried to help any group of humans like that?"

He had a couple of tales, but it sounded like people were helped as a side effect of his own needs.

Jason growled, "Humans don't deserve my help. They should have appreciated the breathing spell the Plague brought."

"Ha! You're irrational to expect people to appreciate their own slaughter. People don't normally look forward to their own genocide."

"Well, there's culling and there's genocide. Nobody knows the difference. I certainly do!"

She laughed. "Delusional!"

He frowned. "I know exactly what I'm talking about! You don't know anything about the people that created us! I wiped them out, genocide if you will."

Facing the Past

"Attempted genocide!" She yelled at him. "You're so full of yourself that you didn't even check on them."

Jason looked shocked.

She glared at him. "Life Force Technologies, a genetic research group in Australia created us—Alpha and Beta. When the genetic purge happened they rushed to escape, leaving the two infants in foster care."

Gina continued the summary, telling of their escape to space, on the Alexandria habitat. She was just repeating the words he'd told Paula Campbell centuries ago, but she steamrolled over his stunned silence.

"And that's when the original Beta, calling herself Dr. Bet Nomad, discovered the genetic trait that was causing infertility among the Alexandrians. She was so incensed by the evil of the weapon used against them that she created a treatment to restore the fertility in an adult female. Then when the group survived the Plague, they made it part of their culture, growing into a secret, literacy-worshiping group that migrated to Luna, now calling themselves the Alpines.

"Since then, they've thrived and produced the Alpine Society, focused on the betterment of humanity. Now, they've spread out all over the known worlds. Not even you could track them all down and kill them now."

He was shocked. He stood up and paced across the width of the cabin.

He turned to her. "You say they're a secret group. How do you know of them?"

"Who do you think discovered Beta-1's remains in your secret lab and cloned me?"

"How did they find it?"

"You may be smart, but enough ordinary people asking questions can find out things you thought hidden. Sometimes you're sloppy. You can't keep a secret a hundred percent of the time."

"But—"

"A woman named Paula Campbell captured you and injected you with a truth serum and you blabbed all your secrets to her."

"She died!"

"Yes, but she was in charge of your computers at that time and the conversation was recorded. I've heard it all."

Old memories were hitting him hard. "The Plague hit. I tried to rescue Beta, and then … I lived under alternate personalities for a long time. I guess I never scrubbed that data."

"Alternate personalities? Alternate identities?"

"More than that. I didn't even know who I was. In many of those personalities I believed I was human."

"Multiple personality disorder?"

"Not that simple. Yes, with the loss of the first Beta, I was fractured, but I'd perfected the art of disguise by losing myself in alternate identities. Jason is not my true self, although he's pretty close. At all times, there are at least three identities that I can count on.

"There's who I call the Old Man. He's my ancient self, but never walks and talks, he just watches and sometimes forces a switch in my personality. He's not happy at how open I've been with you.

"There's the Warrior. He can't talk. He just fights, and he's very good at it. When all else fails, the Warrior comes to the fore and makes sure I survive.

"Then there's the Kid. He's my primary personality, the architect of the Plague and the genocide of the descendants of Life Force Technologies.

"Time and time again, Kid has been truest version of me. But Kid was lost for hundreds of years when Beta died."

Gina nodded. "Kid tried to be Beta-2's father?"

He winced. "Yes. And failed."

She considered, "Beta-1 and Beta-3 survived on their own under what human parents they could find, learning to hide and adapt. They lived good lives in spite of it all. Beta-2 couldn't adapt to the conflict of being raised to be your mate, and didn't have the human role models to pull her through it."

"I was raised by people who knew what I was and loved me anyway. I have a huge extended family—nearly all descendants of Life Force by the way. I've done pretty well thus far and I can even tolerate you, most days. I was afraid I would totally despise you, based on Beta-2's life story."

"It sounds like you despise me."

She nodded. "You've done some pretty despicable things. I haven't forgiven you for a lot of it. The real question is, can you forgive the human race?"

He frowned. "I would think the practical question is, can the human race forgive me."

She shook her head. "Forget about that. The man who created the Plague will never be forgiven. Not even among the Alpine Society will the man who tried to wipe them out likely be forgiven.

"For one thing, you probably don't even regret your actions. There are individual saints who might forgive you, but your position in history as the greatest villain who ever lived is secure."

He nodded, frowning. "I had come to that conclusion a long time ago. My only choices are to hide, or to die."

"Wrong."

He obviously didn't believe her. "What do you know? You can't be that old."

She nodded. "Yes, you must hide. Kid can never reveal his history, but there are only a few in the Alpine Society who know who you are, and they have kept it quiet for a long time now. More know about the villain who cursed the Alexandrians than the villain who caused the Plague and only a handful know they are the same man."

"So if I must hide, why did you say I was wrong?"

"Because that's not all you can do. You can change. You can be a force for good, rather than death and destruction.

"Forgive the human race for moving beyond your attempt to control it.

"You tried to be the emperor of a destroyed world with nothing more than few hunter-gathers to worship you, but they didn't buy that destiny. Accept it. The human race is more resilient than you imagined and the universe has more surprises than you can predict.

"You've got great experience in moving behind the scenes and getting people to do things. You've already burned your chance to be a leader, beloved by all, but you can still help the human race in many ways, still staying in hiding.

"You have also abandoned your merpeople. You have the opportunity to edge them from their isolationism. Help them to become a Galactic people as well. They have great opportunities they're ignoring.

"And you should forgive Life Force Technologies for creating you."

He shook his head, sighing. "That's a lot. I'm too old to change."

Gina shrugged. "Like I said, you can't ever expect forgiveness in return, but you could at least forgive them and do your best to heal the Alpine curse. They have the treatment Beta gave them, but like you, they long to be just a part of the human race like everyone else.

"You said to Paula Campbell that their disease was partly based on your DNA. Genetic expertise hasn't come back to the level it was during King Thomas's War, but Alpine Society researchers hope that with our DNA they might discover the cure. You could give them that."

Jason said, "They had your DNA to clone you, they didn't use that?"

She shook her head. "They said it wasn't ethical to use it without permission. They cloned me to get that permission.

"I said it needed to be the both of us. That's why I'm here."

He looked puzzled. She wasn't sure he understood the ethical problem.

Gina said, "So that's it. I need you to change. Because if you can't change, then the very best thing for us to do is aim this shuttle at the heart of the Pit and boost at our highest acceleration."

"What? We'd die!"

"Yes, and if you're still the Kid that can nearly wipe out the human race and curse your enemies to extinction, then the very best thing I can do with my life is to take you with me to the Pit. I'm in my fourth incarnation, after all. Two out of three times, I've been heroic. I think I can manage this sacrifice as well."

. . .

Theodore Barclay, Eldest of Men of the Alpines was struggling through an endless stack of paperwork when his computer chimed. Like many times before, he didn't notice. His hearing was very poor.

Homer Pickering, his live-in nurse, frowned and walked over to Theodore at his desk. "Sir, I believe you might have a message."

The Eldest looked up, startled. He practically knocked over his chair when it the screen showed that the message was from Bethany.

Grandfather, enclosed is the design of a cure for the Alpine curse. I have made contact with the person who designed the curse in the first place, and I convinced him to change his mind.

He still had access to genetic tools and his original design and although it took him two months, he created this drug that will deactivate critical portions of the genetic code and halt its ability to infect others.

I've gone over the design myself step by step, just to check that it would do what he said it would. Your genetic sequencer should be able to construct this drug from the instructions I've included with this message. All Alpines should take the drug. All women will still need the classic treatment to restore fertility, but their children should have no taint of the disease. Within a generation, the curse will be gone.

On a personal note, I will not be returning. I am needed here. I will probably be needed for a very long time. Don't look for me.

Theodore put his hand to his forehead and prayed for her. It sounded like that demon still lived, but she had hope that she could control him. That wasn't a fate he would wish on anyone.

But it was time to pull together all the genetic experts he could find. They would need to do their own checking. As much as he loved Bethany, he couldn't trust that she wasn't fooled.

Still, they would check and test and hope that their long curse was ended. "Bethany," he whispered, "please have a good life."

...

Homer watched from the doorway as the Eldest gathered his strength and began calling his assistants.

Although it would never show on his face, Hodgepodge was satisfied.

The project to pacify the most dangerous man in history had been very high in his priorities. Although it was impossible to predict how people would react in detail, he had even more patience than the immortal variants humanity had birthed. With a few nudges, things had worked out.

It had been a risk to put one of his artificial human bodies to work here in the middle of the Alpines, but monitoring this long term plan had been essential. Seeing this positive result had been worth the risk. Homer walked out to take care of his other duties.

The End

The Project Saga

Star Time

U'tanse of Ko Branch

Kingdom of the Hill Country
Henry Melton

Tales of the U'tanse
Henry Melton

Earth Recovery Branch

In the Time of Green Blimps
Henry Melton

Free U'tanse
Henry Melton

Captain's Memories

Secrets of the U'tanse
Henry Melton

Power of the U'tanse
Henry Melton

Alpine Duty

The High Ones

Alpine Destiny

Lunar Alpine Trilogy

Children of Earth Trilogy

Children of Earth Part One
Henry Melton

Children of Earth Part Two
Henry Melton

Children of Earth Part Three
Henry Melton